OFF

THE

GRID

By Cirrus Farber

To my children

Madelyn, Lachlan, and Grayson

and to my husband and best friend,

Dawson.

I am the luckiest girl alive to have you as my family.

I love you.

Chapter 1

"You have only yourself to blame," my mother whispered to me through gritted teeth as she stared at me over the stack of steaming pancakes. "If you had only done the chores that we all expect of you, you wouldn't be in this situation."

"Fine, you can have my pancakes. I will make some more once I get some butter."

"Suits me just fine," she retorted, "since I am happy with just the maple syrup we made last spring." Well, good for her. As for me, I loved my pancakes dripping with butter, and with all that we'd given up over the last 3 years, I wasn't about to give up the modicum of normalcy that a simple buttered breakfast could make me feel.

Pushing my chipped china plate across the scratched farmhouse table, I resisted the urge to smack my mother when I saw the slight smirk emerge on her lips. "Well, thanks for cooking breakfast for the family. You know we all count on each other to pull their own weight around here, and we try to stay grateful for each other's efforts." Out of view, I rolled my eyes at my mother's words, as I slid on my worn sheepskin slippers and wrestled my arms into my dad's old wool cardigan sweater.

"I'll be back in a bit, just need to get to work on some butter so that I can enjoy my breakfast, too. See you in two shakes of a lamb's tail." Letting the screen door slam behind me, I hustled out of the warm kitchen across the yard to the barn.

There's something magical and mystical about a barn first thing in the morning, a quietness that is unexpected amidst so much life. But, as I squeaked the big doors open, the animals all stirred in their stalls, staring at me over their battered boards. They would have to wait; I knew they were waiting for their breakfast, too, but sometimes it just felt good to be selfish every once in a while, and I was going to eat first today!

"Hey, girl," I patted the nearest cow on the head, "just need to get a bit of milk quick. Just for my breakfast. I'll be back to finish milking and feeding you later." I grabbed the three-legged milking stool from the corner with one hand, and tossed it under Becky's udders. "No, no, no," I nudged the little tabby cat away, "it's not time for your breakfast either. Is it so wrong for me to just want something special for myself? I'll give you some milk after I've had my pancakes!" Squeezing Becky's udders, I squirted a quick stream toward the cat which it caught deftly in its mouth. "You're lucky I'm a softy." Stupid cat.

The tin pail's milky echo filled the barn with white noise, and as the bucket sounds faded, I knew that I had enough to make my butter. I gave the cat a quick scratch under the chin and laid my head between Becky's eyes as she lowed at me. "I will be right back, sweetie. Don't you worry."

The sun was a bit higher in the sky and blinded me as I headed back toward the house. Careful not to let the screen slam this time, I reached up on the windowsill and grabbed a mason jar that tinkled with a few marbles. Aside it, a few blown out speckled eggs wobbled and a nearby pheasant tail nearly took flight.

I unscrewed the jar lid, took a sniff to make sure it smelled clean, poured the fresh warm milk in, and screwed the lid back on, extra tight.

"Hey you, Mom said you were Grumpy Bear this morning. What's up?" My brother Charlie gave me a quick tickle under my ribs, his eyes still fogged over from sleep.

"Don't you ever just want something the way you want it? Like the way it used to be?" I said to Charlie. "I don't know, I was just feeling annoyed. I mean, is it a crime to want to have some freaking butter for my pancakes? And mom was so high and mighty, talking about all of us doing our chores. So, yeah, I forgot to make the butter this week, and I know it was my job, but really, does she have to always rub our noses in this stuff?" Charlie sat down to his plate of pancakes as I leaned up against the door, shaking my jar of milk, the marble tinkling inside like the ticking of a clock.

"You know how she is, all about learning responsibility, blah, blah, blah," Charlie said, making air quotes in the air around the word responsibility. "But Rose, you kind of are surprising me a little bit."

"What do you mean, I'm surprising you?"

"Well, in your desperate effort for butter for your pancakes, to make like things are all seemingly normal in our life, I guess I was just surprised that you were kind of being stupid. Okay, not stupid, just kind of ridiculous and not really thinking." Cutting off a big piece of pancake, Charlie folded it upon itself, whisked it around in his pool of syrup on his plate, and chomped the big bite, letting his words sink into my head while his breakfast sank into his belly.

He is so lucky that I actually like him. I mean, for a brother, he can be a bit like a smarty pants at times, but he generally does not get super high and mighty. "What wasn't I thinking about, what was ridiculous?" I asked him, tickling him back while he was cutting another bite on his plate, making him splash his syrup onto the table.

"Seriously?" He paused and honestly thought that I was going to read his inner thoughts. "You can't see how you are being just slightly stupid?"

"No. Enlighten me, my brainiac brother." I shook my jar at his head, keeping time with the marble and humming the Jeopardy theme song like he was a contestant on the old game show and the timer was about to buzz.

"As smart as you are sometimes, sis, when you get crazed about something, you just don't think." He grabbed the jar out of my hands and shook it right back at me. "The butter? Really? How were you going to make it from fresh milk? You have made it so many times during these last 3 years! You know you need to use the cream that has floated to the top after the milk has cooled down! You would have just shaken that jar forever, and just finally gotten tired. I mean, I get it, you wanted butter, but think about what you are doing!" He gave the jar a final few shakes and put it down on the table, the marble shushing around and around inside until finally coming to a stop.

I sat there in silence for a few seconds, letting what Charlie said sink in. Not only was I jerk, but I was a stupid jerk. "Awesome. So, now in addition to be a jerk, I am also just plain dumb. I'm sure this development was exactly what Mom and Dad had planned when we moved out here to the farm. Guess, as hard as they've tried, they can take the girl away from the jerks, but they can't take the jerk away from the girl."

Charlie sat quiet for a moment. The wind blew the screen door open, only to have that same wind slam it shut loudly a few seconds later.

"Listen, this is our life now. Get over it. You can either wish and wish that we were back in our old house, our old neighborhood, our old school, with our old friends and just make yourself miserable, or you can just deal with it and make the most of it. Maybe just try to see the glass as half full once in a while."

I chuckled and picked up the jar, giving it a little shake. "Well, you know what? I can do even better than that. I may not have any butter for my pancakes, but I do have a glass of fresh milk." I unscrewed the lid and took a big gulp. "There. How's that for half full?"

Chapter 2

"I'm not really sure how you can manage to make a 48 point word from 3 letters. I am lucky if I get 10 points from 5 of my tiles!"

My dad gave my knee a playful squeeze as he rose from the couch to load a few more logs onto the fire. As the logs settled into their new spots, the fire danced upward, twirling about like a ballerina pirouetting across a stage.

"If you had been playing Scrabble for as long as I have, you'd be able to get just as many points. Like just about anything else, it takes practice, and of course, a bit of luck. Luck always helps." He reached into the game box, shuffling up the wooden tiles a bit before grabbing three and placing them onto his rack.

"Well, clearly then, I am just not as lucky as you," I said matter-of-factly.

"That's not true, but you just don't practice enough to be able to take advantage of luck when you are actually in its presence!" He settled back onto the couch next to me, and leaned over to give me a peck on the cheek and peek at my letters. "See, you have A-S-P on your rack, and you could have played that right here! An easy triple word score! Best three letter synonym for a snake that there is!"

"Don't look at my letters, Dad! That's not fair, you cheater!" I grumbled, nudging him away from me with my elbow.

"Oh please, I was just trying to help. It's not like you would have won anyway!"

"Thanks, Dad. Really nice. Way to encourage me. Who uses words like "ASP" anyway?"

"Well, winners use words like that," he giggled, but quickly quieted down when he saw my eyes welling up. "Okay, okay. If you are so upset, just put those tiles back and draw some new ones. Let's see you outsmart luck and your dear old dad," he pleaded. He reached into the box and shuffled up the tiles again, glancing up at me, batting his eyelashes like he was some 1950s film actress, trying to make me laugh.

It was hard to stay mad at him, though I really did try to sometimes. It's not that he ever said anything different than my mom, he just said them differently. For whatever reason, just the way he said things made me less likely to fly off the handle. Which sometimes, even that seemed like a major accomplishment.

I pulled the tiles off my rack, shuffled the other letters about in the box, drew 2 more tiles, and smiled devilishly at my father. "Finally! I've actually got something to work with, and with this gem, I might even finally win against you! You're going down!" I eyeballed my tiles; I didn't have squat, but I had to make him sweat just a bit. Even if he knew he could win, he liked to be badgered a bit while he was playing. Said it made it more fun. Made winning even sweeter when he thought it was a close game.

"What's the score so far?" My mom entered the living room, bringing the draft from the kitchen with her in her wake. Carrying her knitting basket on her arm, she settled in on the couch next to Dad, tucking her feet underneath her. "Dare I ask who's winning?"

"Well, to be fair, I haven't exactly been the most honorable player. Let's just say that I've admitted to wandering eyes, just a bit anyway." My dad gave me a little wink.

"Well, to be fair, we all know that you would win anyway, even without the wandering eyes. You'd win anyway, even if you were blindfolded!" Hopping up a bit onto my knees, I playfully covered his eyes with my hands, pushing him up against the back of the couch and giving him a tickle as I settled back onto my chair, giggling like I was six years old instead of double that.

Many nights recently seemed to unfold like this. The fire blazing away while Dad and I played a game, ribbing each other all night like we were brother and sister, not father and daughter. Mom knitting on the couch, her presence really only registering through the rhythmic clicking of her needles, like a secretary at her typewriter. And my brother, sometimes helping with the fire, bringing in wood, or sometimes even holding the yarn between his calloused hands so that it could be rolled into balls. But lately, more often than not, tonight included, Charlie was just reading quietly tucked into bed, cleverly removing himself from any tussles that might ensue between the rest of us.

As I cleaned up the aftermath of the Scrabble game, I glanced up at my mother's face. She was a pretty woman, even without make-up, and though I hated it about myself, I secretly liked it whenever anyone said that I looked just like her. Not that there was anybody to really say that anymore, except for my dad. And when he did say that, he got all teary-eyed, and usually pulled my mom and I in for a double hug, like he was the cream inside our Oreo cookie sandwich.

A log fell through the grates, throwing a few sparks up the chimney. "Hey, I didn't mean to lose it this morning," I said, seemingly to the room. " I guess I just got a case of the coulda-woulda-shouldas. Coulda had butter if we were still at home. Woulda just ran to the store if we were out."

"Shoulda thought about how to do something right," Mom whispered from her perch on the couch. "Your brother told me what happened," she said with a wink.

"Yeah, yeah, let's not make it a Rose Bash, okay? I'm trying to say sorry, for Christ sakes." I picked up her knitting, putting my head on her lap, and covered my face with her knitting like an ostrich burying its face in the sand.

Mom lifted the knitting, peeking at my upturned face. "Okay. No Rose Bash tonight. But, not to change the subject or anything, but we do need to start planning the real Rose Bash. Your birthday is coming up, and it's a big one." Without constant calendars and newspapers around, I had almost forgotten. Almost.

Crawling out from underneath the knit blanket-in-the-making, I sat up. "Yup, nearly a grown-up. You'll have to start taking me seriously now."

"And you'll have to take on a few more chores," my dad chimed in. "If you want to be treated like a grown up, you'll need to take on the responsibilities of one."

My mom raised her eyebrows at Dad, and gave her head a shake. "But first, a party. Every 13 year old deserves a party to mark their entrance into true teenager-hood."

"Thanks, Mom. A party sounds fun." I put my feet up on the table, trying to play cool, trying to look grown up and relaxed.

"And then, of course, we'll need to talk about you becoming a woman. About the changes that your body is about to undergo."

"Really, Mom! Don't even start! I cannot handle this right now!" Picking up a pillow from the couch, I chucked it at my mom as she chuckled quietly.

"Dammit, Rose, you made me drop a stitch!" she gritted through her teeth as she picked up her knitting needles from the floor. "I was just joking around with you. Don't get yourself all in a tizzy!"

"Well, sorry about your knitting, but frankly, you deserved it with that last comment."

"Alrighty girls, head to your corners," my dad pantomimed a boxer's jab as he lifted the yarn ball back onto the couch. "Let's call a truce, shall we?"

I glared at my mother through squinty eyes as she did the same to me. When I saw the corners of her mouth begin to turn up into a slight smile, I did the same right back at her.

"Fine. Truce," I said quietly under my breath. "But let's get back to that party idea. What exactly were you thinking?"

My mom leaned back slowly on the couch, settling into the nook of the arm of the couch, and readied her needles for knitting the next row. With a few tugs on the yarn ball, the needles started clicking away like tap dancers practicing their routine in the studio. From over the top of her nimble fingers, she raised her eyebrows in anticipation.

"Well, I was thinking that we could really go all out, make the day extra special for our girl. First off of all, we'd make all the foods you love- from carrot cake with cream cheese frosting to mushroom ravioli with brown butter sauce to chicken fingers with barbeque dipping sauce. We know our girl and what makes her happy! How does all that sound?" I could tell from her eyes that she was excited about the prospect of making me excited. She was obviously trying to sell this idea to me, trying to make me think that, even though things weren't like they used to be, things could still be good, still be considered pretty damn awesome for a birthday.

"Okay, okay," I agreed, much to my own chagrin. "That does all sound terrific, and yes, super delicious. And trust me, I know how long it's going to take to pull all of that off so that it tastes like the old days. Honestly Mom, wouldn't it just be easier to hike into town, buy some supplies, hike back, and then cook it up quick and easy? I realize that it's my 13th birthday and all, but I'm not really sure if I am really worth all that effort."

The fire crackled a bit, sending a few sparks out toward the rug, but the sparks were underachievers and didn't manage to clear the brick hearth, burning out quickly.

I continued, "Seriously, the homemade barbeque sauce alone will take 2 days, and do we really want to use up our tomato supply for a few cups of sauce? I know you want to make my birthday special, but I don't want to be to blame when there's virtually nothing left in the root cellar in February and we are only eating venison jerky and bread."

"Please, we are not going to use up all of our stores, even though it is a special occasion," my dad interjected.

"But really," I countered, my voice getting louder as the ideas came to me, "while we are in town, we could really stock up so that this winter would really be much easier for all of us. We could really relax knowing we had plenty to get us through."

"Now Rose," my mother started, the voice of reason sounding kind of grumpy, "you know the rules. If we ever did indeed consider buying supplies, Dad and I would go, not you or your brother. The whole reason we decided to live this way was for the good of the two of you."

I could sense a fight brewing. Taking a quiet deep breath, I tried to rationalize with her. "Mom, I didn't say that I would be going to town for party supplies, though you know that really, that would be the very best gift of all."

"You can't always get what you want, you know. Getting everything you want spoils a person. "

I let the silence linger a few moments, interrupted only by the clicks of her needles and the sparks from the fire.

"Mom, don't you think I've learned my lesson by now. I mean, it's been 3 whole years. Haven't I been punished long enough?" I could feel the tears starting to well up in my eyes, threatening to spill over like a mug too full of coffee.

"It's not about being punished. It's about being safe," she whispered under her breath. "I don't think I can talk about your birthday plans anymore right now." Picking up her yarn ball, she stuck her needles into its lumpy loops and crammed it all into her worn knitting bag. "Please make sure the fire screen is secure. I am going to bed now. See you in the morning. Night- night."

Well, so much for that.

Chapter 3

If I were to count the number of times I have considered running away, I think the number would simply keep changing since it seems like I consider it every day, a few times a day. Like when I am shoveling chicken poop out of the coop, or when I am scrubbing our clothes on the rocks at the river, or when I am scraping the sinewy sticky remaining flesh from the inside of a freshly skinned deer hide.

During each and every one of these moments, I am reminded about how a) I hate all of these "chores" and b) it is my fault that these chores are now mine to be done.

Three years. In the grand scheme of things, it doesn't really seem like a very long time, but if you were to add up all of the times I have had to do all these not-so-normal chores, it would seem like an eternity. An eternity of butter making, cow milking, and garden weeding. A forever full of chicken plucking, bread making, and blueberry picking.

And sure, the idea of all of these things done as part of a country drive might sound kind of quaint, but if you had to do each and every one of them all of the time, day in and day out, it isn't so appealing. Not so fun. In fact, rather maddening. Hence, the desire to run away.

And run away I might if where I was going wasn't quite so far.

"Your mom just needs some time to calm down. You know that, right?" my dad whispered as he tucked me into bed. He tickled me under the chin a bit, then wiped his palm down the front of my face. His sloppy hand kiss, his trademark annoying dad gesture of love.

"I know, Dad, I know, I know, I know. She only wants what's best for me. She wants to keep me safe. She doesn't want me growing up to be a serial killer. What did I forget?" I sang this list to my father to the tune of one of my old favorite T.V. commercials.

"You forgot to say that she wants you to make her father bacon in the morning to go along with the coffee that you've recently mastered." He pulled the freshly tucked quilt out from under my chin and quickly stretched it up and over my head. Securing it with one hand, he snuck in some quick tickles under my ribs while I was trapped.

"Quit it! I can't breathe, I can't breathe!" I huffed while trying to squirm out of the blanket.

"Shhh! You don't want to wake up your mom! If you think she's grumpy now, she's even grumpier when she gets woken up when she's just fallen asleep!" He retucked the quilt under my chin, and proceeded to tuck it all the way in under my arms and legs and feet, working his hands down my side like he were doing some weird, dorky dance.

"Of course, of course, wouldn't want to wake Sleeping Beauty. Otherwise, she'll turn into the evil queen. Oops, too late," I turned my head to the side, careful not to undo my dad's careful tucking.

Gently, he bopped me on the head. "You'll see. Tomorrow will be a better day. We'll all start off fresh, and it'll be like tonight didn't even happen, I promise." He waved an imaginary magic wand above my head and tapped me on the forehead, like he was a wizard casting a spell to magically erase today.

"But what's a better day? One where there's less poop to scoop or when there's butter already made and stored from the day before."

"A better day is a new day. No expectations. No worries." He leaned in, putting his cheek against mine. I could smell the garlic on his breath, but I didn't mind. Turning his head, he quickly pecked me on my cheek. "No bad dreams, girl. Sleep tight, bug bite."

Blowing out the candle, he gave my shoulder one last squeeze.

"See you in the morning, sweetie. I love you."

"Love you too, Dad."

I just don't love this life.

Chapter 4

That night, I dreamed about my old life. I didn't want to, and most of the time I really found that with all of the farm chores that I did every day, I was so bloody tired that I didn't dream at all. My body just sank into a coma-like state, too tired to think, too tired to worry, too tired to dream, too tired to remember.

I was at school, lingering in the bathroom after the bell rang. Kathy, my best friend, giggled in the stall next to me.

"What's so funny? Did you find something new today?" I whispered quietly, though I was pretty sure that no one else was in the bathroom after the bell. Everyone else seemed to follow the rules, everyone but Kathy and me.

"Oh. My. God. You know how I wrote about "Gail the Whale" yesterday? Well someone else has scribbled back, saying how not nice that was. So I just tacked on, "What? Is Gail being watched over by the Marine Mammal Protection Act?" I could hear her slapping her leg in response to her own joke, a real knee-slapper.

"Stop it! Good thing I am sitting on the toilet, otherwise I totally would have just wet my pants!" I guffawed so hard, I nearly choked. Kathy always impressed me with her witty, smart humor. A straight-A student, she never studied at all, and I really had no idea how she managed to pass since she didn't turn in any of her projects either. "Please," she would counter, "teachers love it when I suggest an oral presentation instead. Most of them ain't complete fools, you know. Gives them less to grade!"

"What about in your corner, uh, I mean, stall, Rose? Any remarks back to your musings yesterday?

What did you write again?" Kathy asked as I heard her unrolling and tearing off some toilet paper.

It kind of bothered me that Kathy could rarely remember specifics about me, but at least she was here with me now. As she flushed, the door creaked open from the hallway.

"Who's still in here?" a voice boomed from the bathroom door. Crap. Miss Lester, the vice principal.

"It's just me, Rose Lee and Kathy. There was quite a line before, and since we just did the mile run in gym and had a ton of water, we really had to go. Our next class is with Mr. Stewart, and he never lets us go!"

"Well, girls, you may have noticed, but there has been a lot of graffiti in this bathroom recently. Mean stuff. And we are all just trying to figure out who's to blame. Got any ideas?"

Mrs. Lester was pretty tough, but I had always liked her. She didn't tend to pester anybody for minor stuff, but she certainly didn't walk away from anything either. There was a time when kids were cutting themselves and posting pics online, and she had made her own Facebook account to get to the bottom of it.

"Hold on a sec, I'll be right out," I blurted out from behind my stall door. As I yanked up my pants, my Sharpie fell out of pocket, and rolled out from under the partition. I flushed, hoping that she didn't notice the telltale evidence on the floor beneath my feet. After taking a big breath and fixing my sweater, I slowly lifted the squeaky latch, shuffling my feet straight to the sink. Averting my eyes, I washed my hands nonchalantly, and then checked my recently applied mascara in the mirror, inadvertently making eye contact with the vice principal in my reflection.

"Is that your marker, Rose?"

"What marker?"

"The Sharpie under your foot."

"Oh. Nope."

Mrs. Lester looked at me with an air of disappointment. "Really, Rose? What do you take me for? Do you think I was born yesterday?"

Kathy's door groaned as she opened it, and she walked over towards me at the sink.

"You girls will need to come with me to my office. Even though you two are typically good students, with all of the drama that has happened in these halls over the last few days, I am not playing any favorites. Get your things and come with me."

She waited by the door as we gathered out backpacks and purses, and though I considered it for a second, I left the marker, my best one, on the floor at my feet.

"Rose, you might as well grab it," Miss Lester said. "If nothing else, I wouldn't want anyone else getting a hold of it and making things worse in here."

Making sure my pants were pulled up in the back, I leaned over, picked up the marker, and handed it to her.

"Just hold onto it for now. I've got some Purell in my office and I'll deal with it there."

It didn't take long for her to piece it all together, find the missing loopholes in our story, even compare the handwriting with tests from our teachers. Suspended for 4 days, I never wanted so badly to just be sitting bored in class.

On the drive home from school that day, Mom was brutal, loud, ruthless, but it was Dad's silence in the driver's seat that really sucked.

"What have we done to raise such an obnoxious, mean girl? Whatever made you think that that would be okay? That hurting someone else's feelings would make you cool? I just don't get it, Rose." My mother's monologue continued, but I could barely hear her, listen to her, through my father's tears. He was crying so hard he seemed to need windshield wipers for his eyeballs, a thought he actually would have found amusing during any other time. Any other time he would have complimented me on my sense of humor, claiming that I was lucky to have inherited it from him, even if I didn't necessarily get his good looks.

When we got home, we all just sat in the living room, staring at each other, not knowing what to say. A slow-moving black fly buzzed around the lamps, eventually landing on the coffee table. People say how loud silence can be, but I'd never experienced its deafening roar until now.

My father was the first to break the sound barrier that had enclosed our family like a force field.

"You know, I've been thinking. A lot. Watching you and your brother deal with stuff at school lately, deal with nasty kids, even be nasty kids, I just don't want it to go any further. You are both at an age when you are old enough to know better, and you are both at the age when you are turning into the people that you are going to be. Not really sure how I feel about my daughter being like this, being a mean girl, when your mother and I have worked so hard to try to raise you right."

The lone fly took flight again, buzzing between us doing its own version of a flyover. Frankly the distraction was welcome, giving us all a focus away from our own thoughts.

"We have talked about this without you, about the possibility of just leaving our lives for a bit while you and your brother were too impressionable. Get you away from the kids who could turn you into the people we never wanted you to be. The world seems to be moving so fast now, and there are so many kids who like to make the other kids around them grow up fast too. Thing is, your childhood is short, and life goes fast enough without having other kids pressure you into speeding up growing up. The technology in our world right now, it seems like there's no way to slow down. You're either completely part of it all or dinosaurs like us. And frankly, we're thinking it's not so bad to be dinosaurs right now. At least we see the people around us, we connect with them, and not just over the Internet, but really connect. We feel what they feel because we care. All this technology, you kids don't even see each other anymore. You just see the words and pictures flashing by you on your little Smartphone and iPad screens."

The buzzing in the room stopped, and the fly dropped dead from under the lampshade onto the side table. I couldn't help but watch his wings tremble during his last moments, fluttering quickly before going completely still. My gaze shifted to my mother, whose eyes remained transfixed on my father. She awaited his returned stare, but his focus was on me, or seemingly beyond me. Not quite looking at me, but rather through me.

"When the time seemed right, we'd always said, we'd pledged, that we would do this. That our family is too important to risk its ruin with just these few tough years. It won't be forever, but it will need to be long enough for you to learn who you are without leaning on the world of Facebook or Instagram to tell you who you are and who you should be friends with. As a family, we've always loved camping, being one with nature and the earth, and sometimes to find greater meaning, we need to leave the world as we know it behind. If anything happens with the two of you, that's it. We're just going to move off the grid for awhile."

My dad has always been a man of few words, and if he had ever uttered this many words at once before, it certainly was only while retelling some long, complicated joke. But he didn't have his deadpan joke-telling face on right now. He seemed to be wearing the mask of a TV evangelist, of someone trying to convince all others around them that this was the way to salvation.

I just didn't know if I wanted to be his follower.

Chapter 5

I awoke with that sweet, happy, foggy feeling. Like you'd imagine heaven, floating weightless on fluffy cumulus clouds, completely enveloped in peace. I wiggled my toes a bit, feeling the crisp, clean sheets against my feet, my toenails a bit too long, scratching against the cotton. Too noisy for my liking outside the window, the birds were making their raucous morning assault on my ears.

"Hey you, time's a-wastin', " Charlie whispered through the crack in the door. "Let's not relive yesterday, okay, Rose? Get your butt outta bed and let's get on with the day!" He raised his eyebrows at me in anticipation, checking to make sure that I would follow suit.

"Is it really so much to ask to just sleep in every once in a while?" I groaned as I rolled over, pulling the covers back over my head. Just 5 more minutes, really.

"If you want to hear it from Mom and Dad again today, then sleep in. I, for one, would just like to have a bit of fun today after chores are done. Looks like it's going to be a beauty of a day." He waited for me. I could hear that he hadn't closed the door yet, and he was making sure that I was going to be available as his sisterly sidekick for the day. "Come on," he beckoned, "as Dad always says, plenty of time to sleep when you're dead." He stared at me with wide eyes, raised brows, and a waiting smile. Humph.

Honestly, I just don't know where my brother came from sometimes. He was just always so unreasonably GOOD, and unfortunately, so freaking nice that it was really hard, nearly impossible to be mad at him. Especially since most of the time, he was right. Jerk.

"Okay, okay. Tempt me. Whatcha got in mind? Cause really, I'm not sure I am ready to leave this cozy nest of a bed just for cows that need milking and weeds that need pulling." I poked my toes out of from under the covers, pointing them at him for effect.

"Well, I was thinking of maybe taking that canoe we built last spring out on the lake for a paddle and going for a swim. Bet the water might be just about right for the first swim of the year."

"You know Mom is going to have a whole extra list of chores for us with such a sunny day. There's no way we'll have that much time."

"Well, aren't you lucky that your brother is so forward thinking? I checked in with her earlier this week and picked away at some of the pet projects she had in mind. I even cleared some land for the new chicken coop!" He raised those fuzzy caterpillar eyebrows of his at me again, smirking a bit. "Consider my good deeds money in our pockets. She won't be able to say "no" now."

I considered his proposal for a minute, relishing a few extra moments in bed.

"Fine, fine, fine. I'm up. Fun sounds much more, well, fun, than chores." I pointed my toes at Charlie then at the door. "So close the door, big brother! Give a girl a bit of privacy while she gets her lazy bum out of bed. As you said, day's a-wastin'!"

Goodbye comfy bed. Hello boring chores. Goodnight dreaming normal girl. Good morning reality country chick. Goodbye electricity. Hello chicken coop.

Another day begins.

Chapter 6

Knowing there was something a little different to look forward to made the chores go a lot faster. It made me think that we should really get into the habit of making solid sibling plans and getting onto Mom's good side so that the drudgery of each day's work would go by faster.

"Hey, Charlie boy," I called across the garden, shaking my stick like an old man shaking his cane. "You almost done planting all those peas? I've got just a few more rows of lettuce. These seeds are so annoying, so ridiculously tiny!" I shook my stick at him again, the one I used to draw the line in the soil to place the seeds so that they weren't too deep and the rows were straight.

"Yup, nearly done!"

I tamped the soil over my last row of lettuce, one of the many vegetables that would sprout out of the ground over the next few months. Though I never much cared for them before, I had begun craving the fruits of the next harvest after all the winter months of potatoes, carrots, and turnips. There were really only so many ways to doctor up the dregs left in the root cellar, and I was ready for the lighter tastes that spring provided.

"I'm gonna run inside and just let Mom know that we're going to head off for a bit, and I'll grab a few snacks for my backpack, too. Any requests?"

"All good, Rose. Surprise me! I'll be all set when you get back out!" Charlie shouted over his shoulder as he bent back down to the dirt.

Carrying my rusty trowel and dusty seed bag back to the barn quickly, I dodged a few scratching hens as I scurried into the kitchen. Mom was sitting at the kitchen table, peeling potatoes and placing the scraps into the compost bin.

"Just gonna grab a few snacks for our canoe ride, Mom. We shouldn't be gone too long, certainly back in time to help with the rest of dinner. "

"I made those apple muffins this morning, if you want some of those. Also, before you head out, have you thought any more about what you want for your birthday? Really, Rose, it is a big one and we want to celebrate our girl." She slid the slimy spud into the waiting colander.

I stared down at the heap of potatoes, trying not to look at my mom. "Honestly Mom, you know what I'd like, and it doesn't need to be forever. But consider it. I am happy with our life, but sometimes I just miss…" I couldn't finish. I could feel my throat start to tighten up, like my heart had filled up my throat, and I nearly choked on my sadness.

I let time stop for just a second, and I didn't even let myself think. There just seemed to be nothing. No time. No past. No future.

"Listen, Charlie is waiting for me, and we are super excited to head out on the water. I'm gonna go, Mom. Thanks for the muffins! They will be a perfect snack for our canoe adventure! We'll be home in time for dinner! Love you and see you in a bit!"

Stuffing the muffins in my backpack, I didn't even care if they got smushed. It was way easier zipping out the door and eating crumbled muffins than facing my mother's eyes. And seeing the disappointment.

Chapter 7

"If you tip this canoe, you are never going to be safe ever again. When you are sleeping, you'll need to be afraid. When you are in the outhouse, you'll need to keep an ear to the door. Though I am excited for this adventure Charlie, I am warning you." I carefully rested my paddle across my lap, turning my head so I could look my brother in the eyes.

"Don't worry, Rose. I am not going to tip you in! It is only April, and what kind of brother would I be if I dumped my sister into the water for the first swim of the season?" Charlie implored me.

"Well, you'd probably be a normal brother if you did that, but since we both know you're not normal, I guess I can just relax!" Giving my brother a hard time about being so good was one of my very favorite things to do, especially knowing he was so good he wouldn't ever really do much about my teasing.

I slowly eased my paddle into the water, watching the little Cheerio rings spread out from the drips. As if I had seen actual Cheerios in the last 3 years of my life. Or even the crinkly plastic bag that held the Cheerios. Or the colorful box with the crossword puzzles on the back that would keep kids from fighting with each other over breakfast. Nope, hadn't seen anything that my family or I hadn't made, hunted, or grown in quite a while. But still, reminders of the past seemed to lurk everywhere, even in the little ripples on the lake's surface.

Carefully I maneuvered my paddle through the water lilies as they seemed to tug gently back, and I headed for open water. As we glided out away from the edge of the pond, free of the lilies, we seemed to coast across the flat calm, silently creeping toward the mysterious depths.

Quietly at peace, the stillness brought calm to my head. Though there was a rhythm of the water lapping at the side of the canoe, it was as quiet as a heartbeat, like it was pumping life back into me.

A bullfrog's croak broke the silence and I couldn't help but giggle. "That big guy must think he is king of this lake; just listen to him crooning to his ladies!"

"Funny thing is, he may think he's all that, but I bet he's got skinny froggy legs! Probably not much of a looker!" Charlie smirked.

"Unless of course, you happen to be another frog! You know the old saying, "Beauty is in the eye of the beholder." Honestly though, even though I'm not into frogs myself, I still would like to see that cocky frog! Maybe even catch him and give him a smooch!" I giggled at the thought and how slimy his little froggy body would feel.

"Wow, Rose, you really are turning into a country mouse. Wasn't sure it would ever really happen, but with comments like that, I think these years have certainly changed you!" He flicked his paddle at me, spraying me with water.

"Oh, I don't know, you can take the girl out of the city but you can't take the city out of the girl!"

"Now, now, wait a second. You say that, but you really have gotten to be really good at lots of the farm chores. In fact, so good that I might even say that you enjoy them!" Charlie dug his paddle a few times backward, turning the canoe so that we could go to my favorite little cove on the lake, an itty bitty oasis with overhanging trees that seemed to create a fort over the water.

"I wouldn't say I necessarily enjoy them as much as I don't hate them nearly as much as I used to. Don't get me wrong, though, Charlie boy. Given the chance, I really would like a taste of our old life again. Just for a day."

Charlie put his paddle across his lap and one end dripped Cheerio circles back into the water. I turned my head around to face him, to make sure he wasn't going to splash me with water, to make sure that he heard me.

"Really? After all this time, you'd still like to go back?" He dropped his chin, peering at me from under his long camel-like eyelashes.

"I am nearly a 13 year old girl, Charlie! Yeah, I want to feel like a normal teenager, especially now that I am almost officially one!"

"Well, I guess we can all have our dreams, but I don't think that Mom and Dad are really ready to return yet. What do you think?"

"Well, they asked me what I wanted for my birthday, and for once, I actually told them. I told them I wanted to go back to our old life for a day. Not forever, but for a day."

"And?"

"No answer yet. I dropped that idea on Mom like a silent-but-deadly fart and quickly jetted out.

Figured it was better to let her digest the idea and then talk to her about it later. Give her time to calm herself down after what surely would have turned into a hissy fit! I'm sure the hens in the henhouse got quite a show when Mom went out to collect the eggs!"

I pulled my paddle up, tucking it into the bow of the boat. I slowly eased my body down low in the seat so that my arm could dangle over the side and I wouldn't tip the canoe. My fingers lightly touched the surface of the water and the water bugs, water boatmen, I think, scattered out of the way. If only our own lives were so simple, just backstroking our way through life, our only worry a giant boat that might push us under the water for a bit, only to pop up again once it had passed, and then just return to our leisurely backstroke again.

"You know, you are probably going to hate to hear this, and I really don't want to ruin our first fun spring day, but I think living like this has made you nicer. Really." Charlie shuffled his feet at the bottom of the canoe, as if he was trying to get more comfortable.

"I mean, you were plenty nice to me as a sister, but there were times when you were, well, nasty. Mean. Cruel. Especially at school and to other girls." He dug the paddle again, facing the boat into the sunshine. "Sorry to say it, but you might as well know."

Do people ever really see their weaknesses? Hearing them aloud from those we trust, for lack of a better word, sucks. It sucks because we want to believe that those people see only the best in us, but I guess really, they want only the best of us, and want us to be our best. It was annoying how good my brother was. Twerp.

"No, don't be sorry. I need to hear it, and I know that I was like that. Glad to hear that you don't think of me like that as much anymore. I'm trying, really, I am. Trying so hard that I hope that someday we can just return and just be normal."

"Well, I hear you. Loud and clear. Though I don't mind playing Boy Scout for a while, there are definitely times when I think, "You know, there are machines that do this now. Why am I wasting my time doing all this? Must we really grind our own flour? Really?"

"At least you feel that way too, sometimes. If you didn't, I would question your sanity. And if you are not sane, then I would be absolutely insane! And if I were insane, there would be no way whatsoever that Mom and Dad would let me go back to reality!"

"Seriously, Rose, you didn't think I thought that way sometimes? I might not be your typical boy, but I am mostly normal, you know! SO normal in fact, I think I am going to tip you in for a swim!"

He quickly reached his paddle far out into the water and pulled hard. I leaned out in the opposite direction, but he threw his weight against the side of the canoe, turning it onto its side, until before I knew it, I had splashed into the water. As I tumbled about,

I finally oriented myself, with my eyes following the lines of sunlight up to the surface. Holding onto the side of the canoe, I looked around for Charlie anxiously, secretly relieved when he sprang up next to me.

Rolling my eyes at him, he smiled back at me.

"You know, I don't like that you think I am such a goody two shoes. I am not always so good, you know," and he proceeded to splash water into my eyes, laughing at me while I blinked away the lily pads that clung to my face.

Chapter 8

Even before I heard the words, I knew what my mom was going to say. Her breath warmed my ears as she whispered, "Happy Birthday, Rose." She gently tugged the covers as she crawled in next to me in my bed. "Scoot over, love bug. You came out of my body; you can at least let me snuggle in close to you one day a year." Every year since I could remember, this is what she did. Came into my bed on my birthday morning. She never forgot.

The sunlight dappled across her face, highlighting the fine lines around her eyes, showing her age. Her whispering continued, "You know, it's my birthday, too. I mean, I also get to celebrate since you were only brought into this world because of me!"

"Yeah, yeah, yeah, I've heard that before, Mom. Thanks for giving me life and all. I know I wouldn't be here without you. Thanks." I gave my words a second to sink in, like syrup on pancakes, sticky sweet.

She waits for me to roll over so that I am face to face with her, our eyes mirror images of each other: same almond shape, same green color, same sparse lashes. She brushes my bangs away from my forehead, reaching up to lightly kiss the exposed spot. "Some days it feels like you were born yesterday. That this has all been a dream, a dreamy foreshadowing of what my life was going to be when I grew up. That I would have a daughter who looked like me and would drive me crazy like I drove my own mom crazy." She raised one eyebrow at me, a trick that I still had yet to master. "Yeah, news flash. Sometimes you absolutely drive me crazy. Like mother, like daughter."

Without my better judgement, I let a giggle escape from my lips. My mom did drive grandma crazy- they fought and bickered like you'd expect from Southern belles in some black and white movie.

"Don't you laugh, missy. If you laugh, you might have the same thing happen to you in your own future: a daughter just like you to make you crazy! Careful or it just might happen!"

Taking a corner of the blanket, she pulled it up over my head, tucking it neatly around my body, swaddling me like a little baby. She squeezed me gently, "Happy Birthday, Rose," and then quickly tickled me around my ribs as I was trapped under the weight of the covers.

"I can't breathe, I can't breathe! " I yelled as the ticking ensued. The claustrophia was engulfing me like a rogue wave, totally out of the blue, unexpected. No time to catch my breath.

Another birthday. Another reminder that I was just like my mom. Another promise that my destiny was determined.

Guess that's what being family is all about.

Chapter 9

"Yes," Mom whispered in my ear as she pulled out of her birthday hug to me.

"Yes, what?" I didn't know what she was talking about, and frankly I was having a hard time reading my mother's mind recently.

"Yes, you and your brother can go to town. For your birthday. As a gift. For the day."

Was I really hearing what I thought I was hearing? Was I really going to see normal life unfold before my eyes- Macdonald's drive-thrus, gas guzzling SUVs, skinny jeans tucked into Ugg boots, graphic hoodie sweatshirts, and Doritos. Doritos, I'd forgotten about the deliciously bad-for-you sinful Doritos. My mind started running, thinking about all the things we had missed these last three years, the food, the clothes, the technology…

"Rose?" my mother snapped her fingers deftly in front of my face. "Are you there? Rose?"

"Ugh, sorry," I said, dazed. "I guess I am in a state of shock. "

Mom pulled me up, slowly sitting up next to her in my bed, fixing my blankets so they weren't so disheveled. "Well, your dad and I talked long and hard about it. You have worked so hard these last three years, and though we want you to want this life, we also know that you miss home. You're thirteen now, and if this is what you want, you have more than proven that your wish should be honored."

"Are you sure? Is Dad okay with this?"

"Is Dad okay with what?" my fathered questioned as he padded into my room.

"Come on, Dad, with me heading into town for the day. You're really okay with that?" My dad shimmied in next to me on the bed, making me the Oreo crème between the cookies of my parents.

"I'm okay with my daughter growing up into the very best daughter that a father could ever ask for. Sure, you've grumbled here and there about our choices, about our new lifestyle, but you've really impressed us. That you can pull off milking the cows when you could barely pull in the anchor line from a sailing day trip before, well, we are just so proud of you. And we are more than okay that you and your brother are so close, for that, we are especially grateful. So, yeah, we're okay with you heading into town for the day." Putting his arm around me, around my mom, pulling us both in close for a papa-bear hug, he kissed my hair. "Happy Birthday, my Rose." He and Mom stood up from the bed, heading to the bedroom door with their arms around each other.

"Time's a wasting! Birthdays are only one day a year, and your day's a wasting! Get dressed for town! Your brother has already taken care of all your chores and is waiting for you!"

Whoa! For real? Happy Birthday to me!

Chapter 10

"Secretly, I am just as excited as you are, so even though it's your birthday, it feels like mine!" My brother clapped me on the back patting me like a horse he was trying to get to go faster. "I haven't really let myself miss home, our old life, that much, it would have just make me too sad. But now that it's happening, I feel like a little kid on Christmas!" He jumped up, clicking his heels together like he was performing a dance number in some cheesy musical. Dork.

Working our way through the brightening forest trail, we barely glanced down at our feet, we knew these woods so well. As we approached a clearing along the path, we both started to chuckle. "Feel like playing house? There's your broom!" As if in a labyrinth, we carefully walked through the pine-needle hallways leading into rooms with beds made of moss. Our old fort. Birch bark blew across the trail, the same black and white bark pages we'd used as pretend menus when we played restaurant.

"Care for a cup of tea?" I asked in my best English accent, lifting an acorn hat off a log table, raising my pinky to imitate a fancy tea drinker.

"No time for tea, now! Maybe we can stop for a cuppa on the way back!" He quickly snatched the cap from my fingertips, pretending to slurp from its rim. He politely dropped into a formal bow, as he hustled me along the worn dirt hallways of our youth. "Birthday girls go first."

"Hey, do you have the list? Read it to me again! Besides the birthday girl's wishes, what else did Mom and Dad want us to get in town?" Charlie adjusted the army green messenger bag across his back, making sure the strap wasn't digging into his shoulders.

I squeezed my hand into my jeans' pocket, and gingerly pulled the carefully folded list from its linty depths. "Let's see here, they have arranged the list based on stores. Guess they figured we might have already forgotten where to find stuff!" I double checked my place on the path, checking my footing. Heading out of the woods into the open meadow, it would be easier to walk quickly in the field away from the roots that tripped underfoot in the forest.

"At the hardware store, we need to get nails, screws, caulking, twine, sauter, a few sets of hinges. Mom wanted us to bring back a toilet seat, but I told her it'd be too heavy to carry in my bag! Didn't want to tell her that it's embarrassing enough to be wearing my mother's jeans, let alone carrying a seat for the outhouse! Not exactly the way I'd like to see my old friends for the first time!"

Charlie's laugh echoed across the meadow like a donkey's bray. "Can you imagine, running into Kathy after all this time carrying that? What would she say? "Hey Rose, looks like life has been treating you pretty crappy!" He channeled his inner donkey again as he laughed at his own joke. "Looks like you've been having a pretty crappy life, indeed."

"Alright, alright. Enough of the potty talk! To get back to the list, we then need to stop at the grocery store. Besides my birthday treats, which I have not even totally decided on yet, there are a few "essentials" that they have requested. Let's see what they have missed over these last three years: hazelnut coffee, sugar, and two bags of Hershey's Kisses. Fascinating stuff, Mom and Dad. You'd think they would want a few more modern day things."

"You know, though, I asked them. They said they like figuring it all out, out here in nature. Off the grid. On their own." Charlie's steps were rhythmic across the field, like the steps you'd imagine the giant taking in Jack and the Beanstalk. Fee fi fo fum, you're my sister, don't watch my bum! I giggled to myself as this silly song rang inside my head. Best to keep my craziness to myself.

"They do have a pretty extensive list for Rods and Rifles, though." The Rods and Rifles was the local fishing and hunting shop. It kind of functioned like the old time barber shops, men just hanging around telling exaggerated fishing stories, about the ones that got away. "They actually included an extra little note to David, the owner. They said he probably wouldn't sell us some of this stuff without a note from them. Said he still might not."

"What's on that list?" my brother inquired, plucking a long piece of grass from the edge of the path and sticking it between his teeth, Huckleberry Finn style.

"Lemme see here. A few boxes of fish hooks and lures, fishing line, a replacement reel, arrowheads, and 2 different types of bullets- shotgun shells and .45 caliber. If I'm as smart as they think I am, I reckon we need the note so we can get the ammo without a firearms license."

"That would make sense. Good thinking. Other than that, they just said we should stop into Top to Toe on Main Street to pick up some new jeans, a few new shirts, and boots. It's my birthday, and you get to benefit. Lucky you!" I punctuated this last thought with a pine cone tossed lightly at Charlie's head. Bull's eye!

"Don't start something you can't finish, oh sister of mine. You know I like a pine cone war as much as anyone!" He whisked my pinecone ammo from the ground and gently whipped it back at my knees. "You wanna call a truce so we can just get on our merry way, or do you want a full on battle?" His eyes twinkled in the morning sun, and I knew I had no choice.

"Truce, please. One for one. Let's just get to town. We are nearly there."

Though it felt like we were so very far away from town, we were really only a 3 hour hike through the mountains. At first, Charlie and I could barely hike a mile, but after foraging for food with our parents, hiking the woods was like walking a busy sidewalk to city kids. You just did it. But over these past years, we had never been back this far. Back this way. Maybe because of what Charlie had said- if we didn't see town, we wouldn't think about it. Wouldn't miss it.

Which is why when we finally saw our town from atop the ridge, down in the valley, we couldn't believe our eyes.

Chapter 11

"What in the world?" I whispered, dumbfounded. "What happened?"

Charlie just stood there and stared at the scene down below, no words seeming to convey what could possibly be going through his head, what possibly could have happened to make such complete and total devastation.

Cars lined up along the streets, doors wide open, everything ripped out from their interiors. Buildings ravaged to nothing- no windows, no doors, wood stripped from their sides. Butchered and skinned like animals fresh from a hunt. And not a soul anywhere. Not even a sound. Just quiet. And not silence like we were used to. Not forest quiet. Unnatural quiet.

I repeated myself, trying to snap Charlie back into the present. "What in the world? What happened?" I reached out to take his hand, more like a friend than a sister. He tugged me in closer, putting his arm around me, pulling me into a side hug.

"I don't know what happened, but it looks like we missed out on some pretty fun times. From the looks of it even from up here, there's been some serious looting happening back in our old town. Looks like we missed out on some crazy stuff while we were busting our butts living off the grid."

"But what could have happened? Why would people loot everyone else in town? What's up with all the cars?" My mind was racing, and I felt like I used to feel when I missed a day of school, missing out on the latest gossip and I had some serious making up to do when it came to understanding the new social climate.

Charlie let go of me, bringing his hands up seemingly in prayer, but really just in thought. "Well, we certainly can't answer that question from up here. Right now, we are just eagles in the sky eyeing the prairie. We can see traces of movement or lack of movement, but we can't possibly know what really is going on or went on down there unless we swoop in close."

A silence erupted between us and the air seemed to breathe deeply, taking on a life all its own. "Up close? It doesn't look right from up here, and it's certainly not going to look right up close, either."

"Well, we certainly won't know unless we go. It's our one and only day we have clearance. There doesn't seem to be any sign of any life whatsoever, so why not? Aren't you the one who was desperate to get back to normal life? Let's check out what we've been missing all this time."

Adjusting his bag across his back, he started down the hill. "Wait a sec. Are you sure about this? I know I was a pain and all about going back into town, but I don't know if I want to go back into town if it's not right. Just not feeling it. Feeling like I could wait it out. Feeling like this isn't the time for a feel-good visit." I looked at my brother, shoving my hands into the pockets of my sweatshirt, imploring him with my elbows and shoulders.

"Seriously, it looks like the damage is done down there. It's like a ghost town- we will just be like tumbleweeds heading down the street, stirring up dust that no one else will see. Let's just see if we can figure out what happened." He turned his back to me and shuffled down the path, as I watched his bag bounce along like the bouncing balls from old time cartoon sing-alongs. Bobbing my head in time with his bag, I froze when he darted out of sight on the trail.

"Charlie? Hey, wait up!" With all the questions spinning through my head, I knew for sure that I did not want to be out here alone right now. Not within sight of the ghost town down below. Not so far from our home. Not alone, not at all.

Chapter 12

My mind raced as I raced to keep up with Charlie on the barely existent trail back to town. Back to normal life. Back to what I thought was normal life compared with the old-time farming existence that I'd been living.

What were we going to find back in town? Where was everyone? Was there anyone left? Where were our old friends? What about our old house? What had happened? What had we missed? Would we be safe?

Would we be safe?

This thought started to run circles around my brain as I struggled not to trip over the stray roots that threatened to make me fall flat on my face. I stopped in my tracks. I pulled my canteen from out of my own backpack, trying not to make a big show of my stopping. Tucking the pack underneath my arm, I rested like I was leaning on a kitchen counter. Comfortable. At ease. Everything except what I was truly feeling. Slowly I twisted the top off, taking a big gulp of water, feeling its cool comfort cascade down my throat. Taking a deep breath, twisting the top back on. Double checking to make sure it wouldn't leak in my pack.

"You alright back there?" Charlie called from further down the trail. I couldn't see him, and for this, I was grateful. I wasn't sure if I wanted him to see the fear on my face, the uncertainty. Maybe we could just go back and tell Mom and Dad that we got lost along the way, that it'd been too long and we weren't sure which way to go, that we didn't know if we'd make it back by dark. Better safe than sorry.

"Yup. Hold up a sec, just tying my shoe." I bent over, tying my shoe as I said I was, if nothing else, just so I wouldn't have to explain myself. Was there any way to turn back now? Did we really need to continue? What if curiosity really might kill the cat?

Settling my backpack between my shoulder blades, I felt its weight against my spine. I remembered whining about carrying my books, that this much homework was against child labor laws. That my back would curve like a hunchback because of this child abuse. I sort of wished this was the burden I was carrying now, not the burden of the not knowing what was down the hill. Of the not knowing if this was all the water I would have to drink for who-knows-how-long.

The path was easy to navigate, even despite the overgrowth. Old snapped twigs showed the way above the trodden dirt trail. The way to town. Been there, done that. Charlie turned his face towards mine as I galloped half-heartedly in his direction.

"You all set? We've still got a bit further to go." He had stopped at a clearing, an overlook of the valley below. At this closer vantage point, the surreal quality of town hung like fog, waiting for it to burn off, waiting for it to all be a dream.

I stared down at my favorite stores along Main Street- the candy shop, the pharmacy, the Whole Foods Store, the coffee shop. The store fronts' windows all spiderwebbed glass like they were decorating for Halloween. Doors torn off their hinges. Garbage littering the street like confetti after a New Year's parade. But this was no holiday. This was no party. This was no celebration.

"Honestly Charlie, do you really think we should go? I am happy to go home, have some fresh whipped cream on strawberries from the garden, blow out my candles, and call it a day. It's all good." I stopped in my tracks for effect, trying to make my point clear, trying to let him know that I didn't need reality as much as I had said I did to Mom and Dad.

"Well, now that we are this close, now we have to go. Now we have to find out. For all we know, we may not be able to find out anything. We might have come all this way for nails and Doritos and we might head home with nothing. We might head home with more questions than answers." He stood overlooking downtown, his carved walking stick in hand. "Blaze Your Own Trail" was carved above the handhold. A phrase that Dad said all of the time, and that Charlie had whittled into his walking stick while sitting around the fire one night.

"Are you sure?" I asked once again.

"If we turn around now, we will forever want to know. Come on, Rose, where's your sense of adventure?"

Chapter 13

It's a strange feeling, that feeling you have when you know you are seeing something, experiencing something that you know is going to change the way you view the world forever. Those things that happen in the world that make the world and reality radically different than it was. Like seeing the T.V. footage of those planes crashing into the Twin Towers on September 11th. Like watching those streams of smoke snaking into the sky above Auschwitz. Like seeing those videos of ISIS beheadings. All images you wish you could unsee, undo so that your mind would not be clouded by the memories of such atrocities.

Walking into town was another scene I wish I could unsee.

As Charlie and I walked out of the forest, the glimpses of town from above were nothing compared to seeing everything up close. Up close and personal.

The conservation area's forest path dumped us out onto the local park. The Little League's baseball diamond. The gazebo where the old retirees would relive their glory in the town band playing concerts in the park on summer nights while kids ran amuk catching fireflies in mason jars and the parents drank too much wine from red Solo plastic cups.

"What the…" Charlie started. Out in left field, a small plane lay deserted, an old crash site.

"What the … is right. What happened here?" We both stuttered, trying to make sense of the wreckage. The plane was on its side, one wing gouged into the ground, wreckage and bits of debris strewn about like wrapping paper and boxes at a kid's birthday party. Food containers littered the ground as well as in-flight magazines.

"Whoa. When did this happen?"

"Well, judging by the dirt, it's been awhile," Charlie said matter-of-factly. "None of this is new. Let's go see what we can see."

Frozen in my tracks, I couldn't even speak. Seeing my hesitation, Charlie reached for my hand. "It's okay. This wreck has been here for quite a long time already. I get it, you're freaked out, but it's okay. Judging by everything else here, I really don't think there's anybody around."

He read my mind. "Anybody alive, anyway. " He held onto my wrist. "Let's go. We'll make it quick. Just check it out." He pulled me along at first, and then I found my footing, my strength. As we got closer, I could tell he was right: this was an old crash. But if it was old, why was it just sitting here, left here to look like a white trash front yard in the middle of our picture-perfect town?

It felt a bit like entering a cemetery. You know that everything there is dead, but it's still creepy, and you can't help but wonder about whether or not zombies were real or if people could actually come back from the dead.

There were no signs of life, but there were signs of struggle. Food wrappers littered the ground, as well as empty pint-size water bottles. Plane seat cushions surrounded burned out fire pits with bits of cardboard boxes left in their charred rings. If a plane went down, why did it look like people were living, had lived, out here?

Approaching the plane's side door, we both stopped in our tracks.

"Ladies first," Charlie said, smiling at me.

"Uh, thank you, but really, I think this time I'm good. Your idea, you're first."

Charlie patted me on the shoulder and poked his head inside. I watched the back of his head like someone would watch a fly they were trying swat, waiting for movement to slow. He turned his head back towards me. "Well, from first glance, it appears as though it's empty." He put his belly on the edge of the door and hoisted himself up to climb in for a closer look. I waited, nervous without him right by my side.

I called in to him," What do you see? Is it clear?" I heard him scrambling back through the plane, finally leaning back out towards me. I asked the question that I dreaded hearing the answer to. "Are there any bodies?"

"All clear. But come check it out." Reaching down to grab my hand, he helped me climb into the wreckage. "Not sure what went down, but there's no one here. Maybe the pilot was able to do an emergency landing miraculously? Hard to tell."

Since it was a small puddle jumper plane, there were only a few seats, and there really was no one to be found. There were plenty of signs of life at one time, though. A suitcase lay open, disheveled and rifled through, a kid's Legos to keep them occupied during the flight left in a heap on a seat. A mountainous pile of pretzel wrappers rose like Mount Everest at the end of the aisle. As we peeked all around, there really didn't seem to be anything there.

"Rose, come see this." Charlie had gotten a bit ahead of me, heading toward the pilot's cabin. As I jiggled the rusty door open, I gingerly stepped over the threshold.

Blood. Like someone had splatter painted the floor with black paint. Old blood.

"Oh. This is awful." We just stood there quiet. A self-imposed moment of silence. Bowing our heads, it didn't feel right to talk, to discuss. At one time, there were people here with lives, dreams. And now there wasn't. All of those lives and dreams had come to an abrupt end. Or had they?

"What do you think happened?" I asked once I felt like I could speak and form words.

"Well, why does any plane crash? That the options are limitless makes you wonder why anyone gets in a plane in the first place. Guess wanderlust lures just about everyone against their rightful thinking at one time or another." Charlie breathed heavily, not like he was trying to catch his breath, but like if he breathed heavily enough, he could breathe life back into the lives that were clearly taken before their time was supposed to be up. There should have been more breaths had by all on this plane.

"Pilot error. Weather. Engine malfunction. Birds. Really, it could've been anything." Charlie started to poke about the remnants of other people's lives. Loads of empty food wrappers littered the floor, strewn about like a teenager's clothes on a bedroom floor.

"What I don't get is, where is everybody? Even if they were dead, wouldn't the bodies be here? And if the bodies were gone, why is the plane still here, wrecked, in the middle of town? I may not be the sharpest tack in the box, but it's just not adding up." I was having a hard time looking anywhere besides the blood stain, like a rubbernecker on the highway watching an accident, completely disgusted with myself. Whose blood is this? Where are they now? Are they dead or did they walk away?

"Chuck, do you think anyone could have survived a crash like this?" Calling him by Dad's favorite annoying nickname for him helped me keep from completely losing it. "I mean, do you think all of the passengers and crew are alive? Otherwise, wouldn't their bodies be here?"

"Honestly, Rose, I really don't know. Let's see what else we can find out. Maybe we can figure it out, maybe we can't. Let's just take a look around." Walking around, I couldn't help but think we were on some old TV detective drama, like we were real-life Boxcar Children solving some mystery. But, I don't recall any Boxcar Children looking at bloodstains. They just seemed to look for ancient mysteries around antique artifacts left in attics. At the moment, dorky artifacts seemed pretty appealing.

"What are these stripes on the walls?" I reached out and over the plane's seats, touching the stripes that ran down the length of the cabin.

"Not sure." Charlie touched the stripe like a blind person reading a Braille page. "They're almost like scorch marks like you would see from a fire or the perfect browning of a s'mores marshmallow."

Looking around for more clues, I beckoned for more information. "What does that mean? It doesn't look like there was a fire. Nothing else here is burned."

"Well, it's like there was some sort of a fire, like something within the walls of the plane. Maybe an electrical malfunction within the wiring?" He asked me like I could answer the question, like I knew.

"Could some sort of electrical malfunction bring down a plane? Aren't there safety precautions that would keep something like that from happening?"

"Well, yeah, there should be loads of safety precautions that should have kicked in if that were the case. But, as we've always been told, things don't always go according to plan. Stuff malfunctions. Accidents happen." Don't I know it.

"Okay, I get that. So let's just say there was some issue with the electricity and power on the plane. The plane crashes. People might die. It would suck. Or people might miraculously survive some crash landing. It's rare, but it happens." I was trying to speak matter-of-factly, but also trying to figure out my own thoughts as I was speaking them aloud. "If either of those were the case, why is the plane still here? Why isn't there some sort of memorial sculpture in its place for the lives lost in the wreck erected here in the park? Since when do people leave a rusting memory of death on their front lawn complete with blood stains inside for added authenticity?"

"Yeah, that's the piece I don't get either," Charlie replied. "And honestly, I'm not sure if there is anyone around to give us that answer, so it might need to remain like one of those unsolved mysteries we used to watch on T.V. But honestly, let's not just waste the day wishing and hoping. All that ain't gonna bring this plane back into the air. Let's head into town for maybe some of your birthday stuff. Maybe there's somebody there with some answers."

I put my butt on the side of the plane and jumped out.

"Answers would be good. And Doritos."

Chapter 14

As we walked out away from the plane wreckage, questions seemed to lead to more questions. Answers were like some elusive species that might only be discovered with years of intense pursuit, but questions were like that pesky mosquito at a barbeque that would buzz about your face that might just drive you completely insane.

Approaching the dusty sidewalk towards town, I glanced back over my shoulder, to confirm that we actually had seen what we thought we did. From a distance, the plane looked like a toddler's hand-me-down toy, simply left in the backyard by mistake when the kid got dragged inside by a tired mother when it was naptime.

"Where do you want to go first?" Charlie asked, deftly popping me back into the present.

My feet plodded along the cement sidewalk, feeling the hardness of society that I hadn't felt through my shoes since we'd moved to the farm. "Not really sure, yet. I say we try to hit the places farthest away first so we are not lugging everything more than we have to."

"Seems pretty reasonable to me, Rose. That's as good an idea as any. And that means we can grab Mom and Dad's stuff first- we certainly wouldn't want to come home empty handed of their requests. We'd be saddled with more chores than ever if we did that!" Charlie jokingly shoved me with his shoulder, making me stumble off the sidewalk.

"Hey, don't make me trip! Not cool!" I said as I shouldered him right back.

"Alright, alright. So, let's hit the hardware store first. We'll try to grab some necessities before we grab your birthday goods."

Rounding the corner, I let out a yelp, like I'd been nipped by a dog. But there was no dog. There was only the sight of town. The sight of devastation. The sight of destruction. The sight of who-knows-what kind of catastrophe.

"Holy crap. What in the world...." Charlie's voice trailed off as his feet stopped in their tracks, suddenly cemented to the cement sidewalk.

Storefronts were smashed, huge plate- glass windows shattered like icicles along the sidewalk. Cars were everywhere- some parked along the street, some in the road, some at awkward angles, looking like some giant had left his matchbox cars out after smashing them all into each other. Even though we'd seen the destruction of town from our hillside vantage point and known that things weren't quite right, seeing it up close and personal and in-our-faces was horrific.

But it was the silence hit us like a deafening gunshot. Not a sound. Not one car's horn beeping, no sirens blaring, no bass thumping as some wannabe cruised down Main Street looking for girls while blasting his wannabe music. Just quiet.

"Chuck, what's going on? What's happened?" My eyes darted to every car, store, window, searching for insight.

"Honestly, Rose, I wish I knew. Between the plane and this, I would say something significant has gone down while we've been gone. By the looks of it, it happened awhile ago, and we are just discovering it now."

We approached the old drugstore, carefully stepping between large shards of glass from the broken windows. Pulling open the door, Charlie called out, "Hello! Anybody there? Is there anyone here? Hello!" His voice echoed off the walls in the store, bouncing like a pinball in the old arcades.

The store was empty, or should I say, bare. Shelves had toppled over or seemed set up in angles like a marble run. Packing boxes were strewn about in the aisles, their contents long gone.

As we bungled our way through the store, I reached for a nearby light switch, trying to shed some light on the matter. Flipping the switch up and down, no ugly fluorescents flickered as I had hoped. "Seems like the power's out, Chuck. We'll have to poke about without it."

Charlie eyed the wall by my hand. "I may not be a genius, but that looks like the stripes we saw on the plane." Just as he said it, I noticed them, too. Skunky stripes running up the wall away from the light switch.

"Another electrical malfunction? Like the one on the plane? I don't get it." I followed the stripes down the wall, up the ceiling, joined by other stripes from other outlets and light switches. I followed the path all the way to the checkout counter, the usual vivid rainbow colors of gum and candies stolen leaving behind a beige metal emptiness. The cash register was wide open, not even a penny inside, but the skunky stripes went down the counter, ending at frazzled bits of wire where the register plugged into the wall.

"You'd think that with today's technology, they'd have some sort of surge strip. That's what those things are called, right? Those long narrow strips to prevent meltdowns if there were an electrical surge, like when power comes back on after a storm? Am I remembering correctly?" Between my fingers, I twirled the power cord, all melted and fried.

"Yeah, surge strips. But that would be here, anybody connected to the grid, not in the air. Not with the plane." Charlie tentatively investigated the remaining aisles, as if he might find a runaway Skittle or hidden Gatorade bottle beneath the shelves. "Damn, this place is totally clean. Nothing here. I don't get it."

"But why is everything looted? If the power went out, why wouldn't stores be locked up tight?

Why the ghost town?" I continued to turn boxes over, as if the answers to my questions might be hidden underneath like a turtle shell.

"Some sort of disaster, obviously. But if it had been a natural disaster, we'd have felt it at our place. But, there's been no hurricane, no nothing. All I can think about is Hurricane Katrina in New Orleans. Remember all that footage of the looting that happened? People stealing everything that they could get their hands on? That's what all this reminds me of."

"But, what would fry the electricity? Why are the cars left for dead in the middle of the road? It's not like the cars were plugged in. Why is the plane fried from the inside out?" I let my questions linger in the air like farts in class. If you cared to notice them, then that was your business, otherwise, they'd just disappear, the truth and perpetrators hidden forever.

With a sense of purpose, Charlie walked quickly to the front window. Peering out onto the scene in town, if he had been in a cartoon, a lightbulb would have lit up above his head.

"You are going to think I am crazy, but I read about something once, when I was doing my science fair project on electricity. There's all this stuff about what might happen to electronics during power surges from disasters, but I remember reading about what can happen during solar flares, too."

"What do you mean, solar flares? Like from the sun?" I had never been the best science student, so I was feeling a little stupid.

"Yeah, as the sun is burning, it sends bursts of energy out from its surface, its corona. Most of this extra energy just spreads out into outer space and the atmosphere, but there've been times when it hasn't. Scientists have documented times when it has happened in the past, but it hasn't happened in a long time. But if it happened again, there would be significant effects here on Earth."

"But it has happened?" Why did I always escape to the bathroom during science class?

"Yeah, it has happened, but a long time ago. I'm trying to remember…. It happened basically before anyone actually used electricity, I mean people used it, but nothing compared to today. It basically knocked out anything that used electricity and fried it."

"What's it called?" Again, thinking now that science class would have been a good idea after all. Teachers had always said that all of this seemingly useless information would be important later in life- geometry, algebra, punctuation rules- but really, I had never really believed them. Until now. Maybe there had been some truth to their words.

"An EMP. Electro-Magnetic-Pulse. A big wave from the sun that interferes with anything running on electrical energy. Stopping the electricity dead in its tracks and anything that might be using it.

I pondered this last statement, dead in its tracks. "Like dead in the air? Like the plane just dropped?"

"Precisely. Like the cars on the road. Dead in their tracks."

We looked about the roadway. Abandoned vehicles, doors wide open. Delivery trucks' back doors gaping like a kid at the dentist's office. Empty.

"Alright, so this E.M.P. takes out all the electronics. Everything that uses some sort of electricity basically just dies. I guess I kind of get it. It's a crazy, rare natural disaster."

"And we didn't know about it because…"

"Yeah, we didn't know about it because Mom and Dad decided that electricity was a luxury that was going to warp our impressionable minds, keep us from being good kids…"

"Yup."

"And since we were living off the grid, we weren't affected. We missed out on this newsworthy natural disaster. By the look of things, it looks like we were pretty lucky to miss out."

"But where is everybody?"

"That," Charlie took a deep breath, glancing around at the cars, the destruction, the desolation. "That is the million-dollar question."

Chapter 15

Wrapping my head around all this science proved to be quite a challenge. I mean, I guess I could get it, but it just seemed so random. So random and so ridiculously outrageous. That something of this magnitude could happen in modern society, it just seemed crazy.

"Let's see if we can find anyone, see if there's anyone around." Charlie traipsed along the sidewalk, carefully avoiding any wreckage or litter in his way.

"Honestly, Chuck, it's like we're in some old western movie ghost town. There might not be any tumbleweeds, but those plastic bags are doing a pretty good job as stand-ins." Peeking in the windows of the stores that lined Main Street, it seemed highly unlikely that we would find anybody, let alone any of the stuff that we had originally set out to get.

"What else is on that list? Even if the stuff is not left in the stores, maybe we can find some of the stuff here in town, on the streets, in the cars, in the trash. Better to come home with used stuff than no stuff. Dad's always telling us to be resourceful, so I say let's see what we can find."

I tugged the wrinkled list out of the back pocket of my jeans. "Nails, screws, all this hardware stuff, chocolate, clothes, and….ammunition." The last word lingered on my lips like a mother's arms letting go of a child before setting off on a big trip.

Charlie let out a sigh. "Hmmm, well, all that's going to be a bit difficult with all the stores looted to their wall studs. Grab one of those sandwiches out of the backpack- split it with me? Need to eat something so I can think."

Swinging my backpack around atop my belly, I carefully unzipped it and grabbed a sandwich from the top. I unwrapped one half and handed it to Charlie. He stepped off the curb, and sat down, landing with a thud on his butt. He sat there biting and chewing, biting and chewing, biting and chewing, like the repetitive action would stimulate his noggin into action.

"Thanks, Rose. Needed that. Sometimes my head gets all foggy when I'm hungry. Feeling better now."

"So what should we do? I mean, really, we wouldn't even be here if I hadn't been so demanding. I'm kind of leaning towards just heading back home, just telling Mom and Dad that we couldn't get any of the stuff. That something had happened and we just baled." I sat down next to him, tearing into my own sandwich half, contemplating my own words.

"Well, that's all fine and good, but really, now I'm curious. Don't think that I am ready to head home quite yet, at least without finding out a bit more answers, or at least seeing if everyone is alright. Or if anyone needs help. I mean, doesn't that sound like something we should check on? Make sure that there isn't anyone here who might need us or Mom and Dad?"

Damn him. He's always got to have some freaking sensible thing to say, the voice of freaking reason. Maybe if I just waited him out, he'd change his mind. Sitting there on the crumbling curb, I zoned out on the sound of my own chewing. To think that I was so freaking close to having Doritos with this crappy sandwich.

"Let's just walk around, check out our old house, see if we can find anyone. And if there really isn't anyone around, I say we just poke about, try to find a few things on the list or at least grab a few things that might be useful modern conveniences for back home."

Shaking my head, I rolled my eyes at my brother. "Fine, but we are not sticking around long. We'll give it the old Warriors' try, but I am not walking home in the dark. That's where I draw the line." Thinking about our old school's mascot made me giggle a little bit, especially since I never had anything that even resembled school spirit. "If we're going to investigate any further, we'd better get going. Time's a-wasting."

And back at the farm, time seemed like all we ever had. Now we were trying to beat the clock.

"You still remember the shortcut back to 93 Baker Street? Race you home!"

Chapter 16

I had thought about our old house so often on the farm- my old school canopy bed, the big comfy chair that everyone tried to snag from Dad nearly every night, the huge red door that I had opened on Halloween for seemingly endless lines of disguised trick-or-treaters. I thought that I missed the creature comforts of home, but I think I just missed the comfort of knowing each and every squeaky step when I was sneaking cookies late night. I missed knowing my house inside and out.

But as I rounded the corner of the well-worn shortcut path, what I saw straight ahead of me was not my house. Not the beautiful house from my memory. And now my memory was tainted.

Charlie grabbed my hand, pulling me to a stop.

"What in Sam-hell has been going on here?" Charlie murmured under his breath.

Our front yard looked like it was decorated for some sort of holiday, but like no holiday I had heard about yet. Some sort of apocalypse holiday. Like CVS had a 75% off sale on ripped clothing, tattered sheets, and old tin cans. Like it was decorated for Halloween, but with garbage instead of skeletons and ghosts.

The front door was ajar, swinging slightly open and closed, as if it were synchronized to our steps. Windows were broken, and if I didn't know better, the whole place looked like a horror movie. The kind of movie where you yell at the main characters for entering such a house in the first place, for being so stupid for going any further.

And here we were. Entering. Just like the stupid horror movie people.

"Are you sure we should go in? Not really feeling the magic right now." I paused to let Charlie laugh a bit at my joke, giving it a second for him to get it.

"Well, magic or no magic, the place looks pretty desolate. It doesn't look like there's been anyone around for a very long time. Let's just go check it out." And just like that, he was heading up onto the front porch. I certainly didn't want to be left behind, so I followed him in like a shadow.

Easing the door closed as I entered, a gasp escaped from my lips. My eyes darted around the house, down the hallway where we used to keep our backpacks, the walls empty of our pictures. It wasn't the emptiness that scared me; it was the stillness. The nothing. The quiet. When we lived here, even when no one else was home, there was a buzz about the place. The fridge humming in the kitchen. The washing machine churning in the mudroom. The TV roaring in the background like the waves on the beach, a constant. And now, the only sound was my quick intake of breath.

"What in the world is going on around here? What's happened?" I said to no one in particular.

"Well, let's play CSI and look for clues." As Charlie referred to an old favorite TV show of mine, I realized that we were indeed playing detective. But as for clues, all I really saw was just one big mess.

As we headed into the kitchen, I was taken aback quickly, not by the mess, but by the smell.

"Ewww, it smells like something died in here."

"Well, who knows the last time the garbage was taken out? Who knows who was even here last?" The table was strewn with empty soup and tuna cans. It was silly of me to think it, but I couldn't believe that someone hadn't taken the time to at least put them in the trash can. Isn't that what civilized people did?

"Do you remember anything about the family who bought this house from us? I honestly do not think that Mom and Dad would've sold our house to them if they had known how they'd ended up treating it. This place is a dump."

"Slow down there. We have to do our legwork. We don't even know if those people were the last ones in the house. Let's just look around some more. Given the state of the town, there's clearly a lot of stuff that's gone down around here that we have missed. Yes, you may have sadly missed Doritos, but luckily we also narrowly missed out on some sort of major disaster. That's what it looks like to me. We just have to figure out what it was, if it was actually an EMP, and where everyone is."

Charlie let his words kind of echo off the bare kitchen walls as he snooped through the cabinets.

"You remember that old nursery rhyme, Old Mother Hubbard? Well, this seems to be her house now since the cupboards are bare. So bare that if they weren't all junky and battered, I would have thought that they were brand new." Honestly, I didn't think that I had ever truly seen an empty cabinet, such a privileged life I had led. Mom had always kept the shelves stocked, with stuff that I swear I had never even seen her use. I remember going through the cans once to gather some stuff for the food drive at school, and some cans had been in there so long that they had gone past their expiration dates. And I didn't even think that canned food could go bad, but Mom said that she couldn't give this stuff to the drive, that even really needy poor people didn't deserve to get our old expired canned corn.

Charlie peeked into the lower cabinets. "Looks like whoever was here didn't just clean out the food. There's virtually nothing left of the pots and pans either. Strange." He opened and shut the doors, looking for anything that might be a clue. Nothing.

"Look at the walls, though." He pointed to the brown tracks, like long snail trails, that crisscrossed along the walls. "I know I can't prove it for sure, but it certainly looks like something happened with the wiring. Like the wires got crazy hot and burned up the circuits inside the walls, scorching the walls from the inside out. That's what would happen during that EMP thing that I was talking about. It would just fry anything connected to electricity." He put his finger on one of the trails, tracing it as a little kid would trace a path in a maze.

The trail continued out of the kitchen, and led us into the living room. Standing dumbstruck looking at the scene, I was reminded of some documentary that Mom and Dad had made us watch ages ago. The movie had been about homeless people and how they got to be homeless, their bad luck and bad choices, and how they managed to survive.

"Seriously. Is this a hobo camp? That's what it looks like to me." The pots and pans that were missing from the kitchen were here, set up around the fireplace. Plates and utensils were strewn around the coffee and end tables, and a large tea kettle sat atop the ashes. As if some big sleepover had happened the night before, blankets were draped every which way on the couches and chairs.

"Well, I'd say someone's been living here, and since the electricity is down, they've been cooking over the fire." Investigating a bit more closely, Charlie grabbed the fire poker, poking about the fireplace. "Whatever they've been eating, they certainly don't leave much for leftovers. There's not a bit of food even cooked to the sides of these pots."

The poker clinked against the bricks and then made a dull thud. Charlie pulled a big log out from the bottom of the ashes, using the hook end of the poker.

"The question is- where are these people now? Shouldn't they still be here at their camp?" He looked into the fireplace, searching for answers. Bending down, he picked up the log. "This is cold. It's been awhile since this fire was going."

"Well, it looks like there was quite a crew here, based on the number of plates left about. Maybe they are out looking for food. Maybe there are others. Everyone else has to be somewhere." I looked around the room, feeling a bit flabbergasted that this was the same room where our family celebrated so many Christmases for so many years. It just didn't seem possible that those happy memories happened in a place that now just looked so sad.

Charlie's eyes widened, and he dropped the log that he'd held to the floor.

"You okay? You look like you saw a ghost."

Charlie stared straight ahead, his eyes on the fireplace. "That was not a piece of wood. That was a bone. And if I'm not mistaken, it was from a human."

Chapter 17

"Human bone? What are you talking about?" As the words escaped my lips, I was left empty, as if the words were actually gas that fueled my engine.

"Seriously. Look at this. It's huge." Charlie held the ashy, dusty relic out for me to see more closely.

I stared at it with curiosity and intent. "Are you sure? Are you just trying to spook me out? As a heads up, the empty streets and looted stores spooked me out enough. I don't need the creepiness increased by human remains."

"Well, I can't be sure, but this is definitely bone. And look at the size of this end joint. It's too big to be a dog or a cat or even a deer, so a person would be my next best guess." He placed the bone into my hands, and I immediately dropped it onto the floor, as if it was still on fire. Using the poker again, he sifted through the ashes, pulling other little bits to the side, out onto the bricks. "See? Here are some other bones. If I were to guess, it looks like this whole EMP event led to everyone going Donner."

"Donner?"

"Yeah, the Donner party? Don't you remember reading that book in 5th grade? It was required reading with Miss Lawry."

"Nope. 5th grade wasn't my best year. Basically gave up reading for texting. Not sure how I actually passed."

"Yeah, if I recall, that's when you really started acting like an idiot. A real jerk."

"Thanks. As if I didn't know already that I was the one to blame for this whole freaking moving off the grid thing."

"Sorry. Anyway, that book was cool. Creepy and cool because it was true. But now as I think about it actually happening in real life, it's really kind of terrifying." Charlie bowed his head a bit, picking up the bone again off the bricks. "Yeah, so, the Donner party was when a whole crew of people were moving out west, back in the 1800s. Fathers, mothers, kids- whole families- looking for a better life. Anyway, they got in the middle of a huge snowstorm, and when their food ran out, people started starving to death. And then, when they were totally desperate, they started to eat the dead, each other. Cannibals." He tossed the bone into the air and caught it. "You really haven't heard of that story before?"

"It kind of rings a bell, but like I said, I didn't pay attention too much that year. So, what are you saying?"

"I'm saying that I think that's probably what's happened here, when the food ran out. That when all the stores were stripped clean and all the cabinets were cleared and no one could get anywhere because everything with electrical wiring had been fried, I'm thinking that people must have started to get desperate. And when people are desperate, they can do things they wouldn't otherwise do."

"You mean like eat people?"

"That's exactly what I mean."

"That's awful"

"That's humanity. People always are desperate to survive, even if it means that your choices mean you'll never be able to live with yourself again."

"Well, if that's the case, I'm thinking that I can live without my Doritos and jeans. And as far as I'm concerned, Mom and Dad can live without the things on their list either. At this point, I just don't want to become someone else's Donner dinner. Let's get outta here."

I put the bone down, and my other hand on Charlie's back.

"Not so fast," a voice whispered from the doorway. "You only just arrived. We wouldn't be good hosts if we didn't welcome you. We'd love it if you'd stay awhile."

Guess we weren't going anywhere.

Chapter 18

"So, tell us again, where exactly has your family been?"

We had been sitting on our old couch, in our old house, looking at walls painted the color of driftwood, a color picked out by our mom, to "calm us when life had us stressed" she had said. Well, if we had ever had a stressful moment, our current situation trumped it. If only Charlie and I could drift away like the driftwood, let the current take us elsewhere. Anywhere but here.

Charlie scooted his butt back further on the cushion, settling in to seem more at ease. He rearranged the blanket again, and I inched my way back, too, and drew my knees up to my chest. Putting his arm around me, he gave me a little side hug. I could tell he was just buying time, getting his story straight in his head, making sure that he didn't say something that would contradict what he had already said.

"Well, when Rose was having all that trouble in school, our parents decided that we all needed a fresh start. So, we moved a few towns away, where teachers and parents hopefully hadn't heard the rumors and stories. We just needed not to be burdened with those ghosts. The ghosts would've killed us all, probably would've made our parents' divorce, and they knew it could all be okay again if we all just started with a clean slate."

Mrs. Russell reached forward for the teakettle on the coffee table. As her elbow brushed my leg, I flinched ever so slightly. Breathe, Rose, breathe. You can't seem afraid. They can't know that you know. You need to be bigger than your fear.

"Would you like a warm-up for your tea, sweetheart?" Mrs. Russell beckoned me with the kettle. "I know it's not what you're used to, but really, is anything what any of us is used to? My old favorite tea was Lemon Zinger- so delicious! I even loved reading the little peaceful quotes on the side of the box. Now, I just have to settle for nettle tea. Not nearly as delicious, but those stinging nettle weeds grow wild everywhere, and their leaves do make a decent cuppa. Good for your tummy, too. They're one of those old Native American remedies, good for just about everything." She stammered on and on, continuing to spout on about the benefits of her nasty-tasting tea. Her voice became like Charlie Brown's teacher, and I didn't hear a word she was saying. I just focused on Chuck's face, on his eyes. Looking for that light bulb moment, I knew he wouldn't show it. I knew that he knew better. And he knew that I knew that he knew better. And I knew that I just had to trust him. And he knew that I did.

"Yes, please. I didn't know you could make tea from those weeds! So cool! I used to hate it when my mom made me weed the garden and those plants seemed to go on attack! They had those leaves that would sting worse than a yellow jacket! Good to know that they're good for something!" Mrs. Russell poured the tea carefully from the ashy, fire blackened kettle, and then got up from her seat next to me on the couch and put the kettle back on the grate over the sleepy fire.

"So, let me get this straight, you moved to escape all of the hubbub surrounding those issues you were having in school?" Mr. Russell chimed in. Sitting in the chair to the left of the fire, he reminded me of a lion overlooking his domain, at peace and calm. But, like when in the presence of a lion, the king of the beasts, one should never, never, never forget, what it truly is. A predator. And we were his potential prey.

"Yeah, Dad wanted to keep his job, keep as many things as possible the same, so that there wouldn't be too much change, wouldn't be too much upheaval for all of us. So, we moved to Easton- just far enough away to escape the gossip and still close enough for Dad's commute." The story melted out of Charlie's lips, sweet and sticky like ice cream- too good not to be true. Damn, for such a goody-two-shoes, he was an excellent liar. Impressive.

"And what about your parents' friends? They didn't think it was weird?" Mr. Russell continued to press Charlie, but Charlie didn't press back. He just spoke like it was all well and good, like life was life, things happen, you move on, and it's all good.

"Honestly, Mr. Russell, after all that Rose did, most of my parents' friends didn't want to have much to do with us, any of us, anymore." He took a big sigh and looked at me, straight on. "Sorry, Rose, but that's the truth, and you know it. I mean, I don't want to say that it was all because of you, but you really were to blame for all of that." Mr. and Mrs. Russell looked at each other and their eyes widened, feeling the weight of the not-so-brotherly-love statement. "Anyway, we just didn't have anything to do with anyone anymore. And even though Dad still had his same job, he wasn't exactly someone who ever really hung out with his work friends outside of work. I'm not even sure if any of them even knew that we'd moved."

Mrs. Russell leaned forward to pick up her steaming teacup and gently blew on her tea before she took a careful sip. "Well, Rose, it sounds like you learned a really hard lesson. But here you are now, here we all are, and the world is a different place."

Rose mirrored Mrs. Russell, and took a sip of her own tea. "Yeah, I just feel really bad for what I did to my family. Even though everything is different now, I still feel really guilty for putting them through all that, making so many problems for everybody." Rose's eyes met Charlie's for a moment, and then she put her head on his shoulder in apology.

Charlie flopped his head on top of hers. "Hey Rose, we all make mistakes. Some of us make bigger ones than others, but sometimes we don't know how big our mistakes will be, how they'll create a domino effect with everything. It happens. What's done is done. Life goes on."

Mr. Russell shuffled his feet, getting a bit more comfortable. "You're right, Charlie, life goes on, and sometimes that's all that we need to remember." He leaned forward to poke at the fire, the flames jumping and licking at the underside of the kettle.

"Anyway, since we were in a new community and all, we wanted to come back here, back home. We hadn't even had time to make any new friends yet, so when this all happened and things were getting bad, we decided to come back here to see if we could connect with our old friends back home. To see if we could find some answers, maybe help each other out." Charlie shifted on the couch and settled back with a confident air.

"What about with you both? What happened here?" Charlie asked. Damn, he was brave. Really, I don't think that I could have stomached asking that question, even as it waited on my lips like a diver on a diving board.

Leaning back into the armchair, Mr. Russell crossed his legs at the knee, a gesture that always seemed to look silly, a bit goofy and feminine, when a man did it. "When it all went down, I had been at work, just sitting at my desk returning emails. All of a sudden, there was a loud bang, like a firework went off right outside the window. And like fireworks, the tops of all the utility poles sizzled like sparklers. People started rushing about, trying to call the fire station, but the phones didn't work. Nothing worked. My whole office ran outside and saw what you guys all probably saw. All the cars deadstopped everywhere. People helter-skelter looking for answers. And then we all got really quiet, dead silent when we witnessed a plane just drop from the sky. Still, just thinking about it, it all just seems like a nightmare, like how could it be possible? As if we've all been waiting to wake up from this bad dream for three years now, and it just doesn't seem possible that this is all for real." Mr. Russell leaned forward, put his face into his hands, and just rested his head in his palms. Slowly he sat back and moved his hands beneath his chin, and for a second, I thought he was praying.

"I totally remember that day. It felt like a movie scene just unfolding before our eyes," Charlie responded. "A terrifying movie scene, and it blows my mind that this is all for real. That our world could just collapse, that airplanes could drop from the sky, it still just doesn't seem like it should be possible."

Mrs. Russell reached out to hold her husband's hand. "And you are just kids. That you had to see all of that, my heart just breaks for all of you, for all of us."

"Well, kids or not, we are all just trying to figure it out now, in this changed world." Mr. Russell rose from his seat next to his wife. "And even us adults, every day brings a new challenge. I wish I had different news for you kids, but I don't."

Charlie nodded. "When do you think they, I mean the government, might start fixing things? My parents haven't heard anything in the way of news in what seems like forever. Have you had any contact with anyone who might know?"

Mr. Russell just shook his head and sighed, distracting himself by poking about the embers of the fire. "Gosh, son, I wish I did. If I did, I might have a little bit more hope for the future. But as of now, I've not seen anyone except others like ourselves just struggling to survive and eat."

I reached forward to take another gulp of tea. "Well, you both have been so kind to us, and we appreciate your kindness and the tea. Really, Mrs. Russell, I like the nettle tea. I'm going to have to tell my mom about it when we get back." I carefully placed the teacup back onto its saucer, as if I were at a formal British tea and not in the disarray of my old home. "And Charlie, we really should be getting back. It sucks, I mean stinks, that we don't have better news for Mom and Dad, but they're going to start getting worried about us. Thanks for everything, Mr. and Mrs. Russell."

Charlie and I rose from the couch and I gingerly leaned in to hug Mrs. Russell.

"Sorry, kids, but you're not going anywhere." I felt a slap on my wrist slapped that was punctuated by a click, and I pulled away from Mrs. Russell's arms, trailing a new set of handcuffs.

Chapter 19

"Have a bit of nettle tea, Rose. You must be thirsty." Mrs. Russell leaned over, and brought a straw to my lips. "Really, it'll make you feel better."

"As if a spot of tea could make me feel better, could make me forget that I am being held hostage?" I snapped. Propped up on pillows, I looked like a hospitalized invalid, not a prisoner, and I struggled against my handcuffed wrists, shackled to the headboard.

"Really, it'll make you feel better. Would I really be offering you tea if I didn't care about you?" Mrs. Russell continued, sicky-sweet. "One can't think straight when one is dehydrated, so let me help you." She leaned forward again with the tea, and I took a slow, tired sip.

It's not like fighting is going to make my situation any better, I thought. I might as well not be thirsty. Perhaps if I am docile and easy, it'll buy me time to figure my way out of this nightmare.

"There, there. That's my girl. Doesn't that make you feel better? Take another sip." I let the straw linger on my lips for a moment before I took another slow sip, draining the cup.

"Thank you, Mrs. Russell. I guess I didn't realize just how thirsty I was."

I had been chained to the bed since the night before, and I was unclear about what time it was now. Was it still the morning? Or had time passed quickly and was it nearly night again? My parents would be a wreck, worried sick about us. They would come looking for us. They would be here soon.

But no. They can't come, I thought. If they come to look for us, to save us, their lives would be at risk, too. I couldn't do that to Mom and Dad; I would never forgive myself. I needed to get free soon so that I didn't put them at risk.

I shifted in the bed, trying to get comfortable. "Sorry, Rose. I know you don't understand, but it's for your own good. We didn't really have much of a choice. All we have is life, so it's what we must preserve, by doing whatever it takes. Maybe someday we'll all understand. Maybe someday we'll all be forgiven." Mrs. Russell nudged herself a bit closer to me on the bed, putting her hand atop mine. "Please know that we have no choice."

I sat quietly for longer than I expected to, but really, what could I say? How could I change my fate now that I was the prey caught in the trap?

"Is my brother okay?" It was the question I knew I had to ask, but I was nervous about the answer. My brother could figure out a way out of this jam, but he could only help if he wasn't already dead, dinner on the plate.

"Rose, don't you worry, your brother is fine. And really, we don't intend on harming either of you, but if we needed to, we just needed to know that if we had to, well…" She couldn't even finish her thought, for to say it out loud would be to confirm her own worst fears for herself, for her future. "What you saw, I can explain. We didn't hurt anybody, really. We just collected people that were already gone. Honestly. If I had been the one dead, I would hope that my life wouldn't be wasted, that someone else might have life if mine was already gone." She poked the straw about the cup, stirring the emptiness slowly. "We're not murderers, it's not what you think. We just were so hungry. So we did what we had to do."

I couldn't bear to look at Mrs. Russell, and shifted my gaze to the billowing curtain at the window, letting in little shining shafts of sunlight. Any other story, this would seem a scene of hope, simple beauty, not the living hell I was currently experiencing.

"Couldn't I see him, just for a little bit?" I posed this question more to the world around me and less to Mrs. Russell, as if asking God to change the course of his or her whole plan, just for my sake.

"Sorry, sweetie, but that can't happen. I think you know that." Mrs. Russell rose from the bed, smoothing out the blankets as she spoke. "I'll be back in to give you a bit of supper in a little bit and to help you use the bathroom. Until then, try to get some rest."

She spoke to me as if I was only sick in bed, a patient with a nurse at my bedside. With Mrs. Russell gone, I would need to use my time wisely and get thinking. How in the world could I get out of this mess? What would Charlie do?

Chapter 20

It wasn't much of a plan, but during the hours that Mrs. Russell had been gone from my bedroom cell, it was the only plan that I had hatched with any hope of success. I turned it every which way in my mind, as if I were turning a shirt right side out, looking for loose threads and pilling, making sure it was ready to wear, that there were no holes that would make for problems later.

The butterflies that were in my stomach beat their wings rapidly, and I felt that if I were not cuffed to the bed, they might actually make my entire body take flight. Too bad that wasn't actually an option.

As I heard footsteps padding lightly down the hall, I took stock of my thoughts. Once I started with this endeavor, would I actually have the guts to carry it all the way through? Had I really thought of all the possible problems that might arise? Would I just throw up from anxiety, the entire plan just thrown out in the garbage, with no hope for myself, my brother, my parents? There was no choice. It was now or never.

The door squeaked open, and Mrs. Russell entered the room carrying a tray. "I know it's not much, but I hope you find the supper edible." She sat down next to me on the side of the bed, adjusting the tray on the bedside table. "It's a simple soup, not much more than a broth really, but I had scavenged and stored some potatoes and carrots from the old community gardens, so at least there's a bit of something to literally sink your teeth into." Given the situation, I thought, it was certainly better than the alternative.

"Thank you. It sounds delicious." I craned my neck awkwardly forward as I tried not to slurp the soup from the extended spoon. Quietly, calmly, I took my meal. No reason to move forward on the plan until my belly was full, or at least not completely empty. I was going to need my strength.

"You know, I know you don't believe me, but we're actually really good people. " Mrs. Russell seemed to be talking more to herself than to me, trying to convince herself that her actions were necessary. "I can remember reading those survival stories in the newspapers and books when I was a kid-hunters lost in the woods surviving on ants, African children eating grubs for protein- and being so grossed out. I mean, I was grossed out eating my grandmother's casseroles if they weren't made with Velveeta cheese, I couldn't even imagine having to eat things that gross." She paused in her self-talk to feed a bit more broth to me, taking the time to blow gently on the spoon so that I wouldn't burn the roof of my mouth. "Now, look at me, look at all of us. I guess none of us know what we're fully capable of until we're actually put into a life-or-death situation. Such is our situation."

I slowly leaned in for another spoonful, and as far as I was concerned, possibly the last bite of any sustenance before I was back home safely in my parents' arms, at their table, remembering all of this like it was only a bad dream.

"You know, Rose, I always thought that I'd have a daughter, have kids, but looking at what's happened to the world, I think I am glad that I never did. I mean, I don't think that I could live with myself knowing that some young kid was watching me, was looking at what I do now. I don't think I could live with the guilt." Taking a dirty handkerchief, she wiped the corners of my mouth, and then turned the handkerchief back on herself, dabbing at the corners of her wet eyes.

"It's okay, Mrs. Russell, I get it. No hard feelings." I looked away from her, feeling bad for this woman. Maybe she wasn't so bad. Maybe her husband was forcing her to do these things. Maybe he was the bad guy.

"That's sweet of you to say, Rose. I guess I just hope that God sees what we're doing and believes that we are all just working to survive, that none of us intended for this to happen the way that it did. Frankly, I don't even know why I still believe that there might be a God. I mean, what kind of God lets his people get hurt this way? What's the point? What kind of lesson is all of this supposed to teach us?" She scraped the bottom of the bowl, spooning up the last bits, and leaned in to feed me the last spoonful. "There you go, sweetie, that's going to have to hold you over for a while. Wish there was more, wish there was more for all of us, but that's all we've got. "

"Thank you, really, it means a lot." I shifted in the bed, tugging at the handcuffs, trying to get comfortable.

"I'm just going to put these things away, let you settle a bit after your meal. Then, I'll come back to help you with the bedpan. Be right back." Slowly raising herself from the bed, she gently patted Rose's legs as she got up. She padded quietly to the door, and let the door click shut behind her.

I counted to ten silently in my head and then let out a big sigh. Could I do this? Would my plan work? Really, what did I have to lose?

As I waited for Mrs. Russell to return, I let myself close my eyes. Behind my eyelids, I saw the animals on the farm, running to greet me as I entered the barn. The musty hay smell quickly filled my memory, and I could almost feel the gentle nuzzle of Becky the cow as she nudged me for milking. Dad's whistling outside filled my ears, and I smiled at the memory of trying to echo his whistled songs, and when I did, he always tried to make his whistles more and more complicated, just to annoy me. How was it possible that they were together just yesterday? It seemed like it had been a lifetime ago.

Footsteps coming down the hall jostled me back into reality, and I adjusted myself in bed. Licking my palms, I smeared my own saliva onto my cheeks and widened my eyes as far as they would go as the door opened.

"Alright Rose, I know it won't be your favorite part of the day, but I'm here to help you with the bedpan. Sometimes, of all things, I miss a working toilet more than anything else." Mrs. Russell shuffled into the room, and reached under the bed for the metal pot.

I gulped, and smacked my lips. "Mrs. Russell, I don't know how to really tell you this, but, my belly is not right. I don't really feel good." I shifted beneath the dingy blankets that covered me, and let my eyes dart around the room. "I mean, my belly's all gurgly."

"What do you mean, sweetheart? You can't possibly be hungry, you just ate." Mrs. Russell settled herself next to me on the bed, clinking the bedpan against the side of the bed.

"No, not hungry, not like that. Like my belly's all…. funky. Maybe it was something in the soup." I grimaced during my description, trying to make my point clear. "My belly's just…. Well." I hesitated for effect. "My belly's just…. I just don't think that I will be able to go in the bedpan. I hate to say this, but, I think it's going to be rather messy." I paused, letting my words sink in. "I wish I didn't have to tell you this, but I figured honesty might actually be the best policy here, better for both of us."

Mrs. Russell set the bedpan down on the floor, letting it clatter to a stop. "Hmmm, well, I do think I understand what you are trying to say. Not to worry, Rose, we've all been there. We've all had that rumble in our belly when we know it's just not going to be a pretty sight." She patted the side of the bed, trying to think. "Well, I can honestly say that I don't want to deal with anything like what you are describing in a bedpan. With no running water to wash up, that sounds like a nightmare to me. Tell you what, let's just sneak you outside so that you can do what you have to do. But you'll need to be quick- Mr. Russell-my husband- can't know that I let you free for even a second." She tugged at the blankets a bit, getting Rose's hands free. "You need to be quick, and then it's straight back into the bed, or your brother is at risk. Seriously." She clicked the key into one handcuff, and massaged my wrist where the metal had left an indentation.

"Here's a rag for wiping yourself. This certainly isn't what any of us are used to, but just do what you have to do." Mrs. Russell leaned in, and unlocked the other handcuff. "Just sneak out the sliding glass door quietly, and squat just outside. Try to lean away from the deck railing so that you don't get any of it on yourself, okay?"

I got up out of the bed, and waddled to the door, clenching my butt tightly as I walked, trying to look the part of someone who might have an accident in their pants. As Mrs. Russell followed me to the door, I grasped at my belly, doubling over in what looked to be pain. Grabbing the bedpan as I was doubled over, I lifted it quickly, and knocked it against Mrs. Russell's head. Thump. Out like a light.

Mrs. Russell tumbled to the floor like a rag doll, knocked out cold.

I scanned the room for anything, something that might be of use to me in my escape, but nothing caught my attention. Grabbing the handcuffs out of her hand, I tugged Mrs. Russell closer to the bed, and quickly snapped them shut, cuffing her to the bedframe. I paused for a moment, and tucked the keys into my pocket.

Opening the slider, I turned, shaking my head in apology to an unconscious Mrs. Russell. "Sorry, but we've all got to do what we've got to do."

The door suddenly flew open.

"Where do you think you're going?" Mr. Russell questioned as he entered the room. Grasping my arm and twisting it like he was in some Kung-Fu movie, he led me back to the bed, eyeing his wife collapsed on the floor. "We wouldn't want you to leave so soon."

Chapter 21

Moonlight dappled the quilt that covered me, and the curtains billowing behind the cracked window made the moonlight dance across my chest. Dad had always called this being "moonstruck", when the light from the moon woke you up and kept you up. Not that I could really sleep, but rest was always welcome, especially with what I had already been through.

So, what now? I thought. Where is Charlie in the house? Has he come up with a plan to come help me? And how could he even help me since I am again locked to this bed? Hope had never seemed so far away as it did right now, but what else could I possibly do now except hope?

I let my eyes focus on the moon, trying to find peace in its beauty, like the man in the moon might just find some magic solution and beam it down to me. Wisps of clouds passed over the moon slowly, and I drifted slowly back into sleep.

Not sure how much time had actually passed, I woke with a start. What was that? I heard something in the night, unfamiliar. There it was again. A tap, tap, tap at the window, and then the window slowly squeaked up a crack from its sill.

"Psst... Rose?" a whisper came from beneath the glass. "Don't be frightened. Stay quiet. I'm here to help." Was this a dream? I shook my head a few times, trying to make sense of what was happening. "Just trust me."

"Who's there?" It wasn't Charlie's voice, and it didn't sound like my parents.

"It's me. Gail, from school." The voice continued from beneath the window. "Remember me?"

My heart dropped in my chest, and a lump caught in my throat. "Of course I remember you. Are you okay? What's going on here?"

"There's not time for that. Just listen. I can help you, I can help your brother," Gail whispered.

I looked at the window, trying to get a glimpse of the familiar face, but the dark made it an impossible task. "I don't understand. How did you know we were here?"

I heard Gail take a deep breath. "Look, there isn't time. Let's just say that I noticed you and your brother come into town from the hills, and since you hadn't been here to witness everything that had gone on here lately, I followed you from afar, just waiting for my chance to help. To help before it was too late."

I gulped for air like I had been underwater for too long, trying to catch my breath.

"Listen, will you let me help you? Can you stay quiet?" Gail posed the questions, waiting quietly in the moonlight for a response.

"Will we be able to help my brother, get him free too?"

"There are no guarantees, but we are certainly going to try. I've got a plan, and one thing I know for sure, he won't get free unless we save him." Gail left this thought for me to ponder.

The moonlight continued to move like a flashlight beam across my body in the bed. "Well, if you put it that way, there doesn't seem to be a choice. Not sure why you are helping us, putting yourself at risk, but also not sure that there's time to talk about it right now. Time's a wasting. I'm in."

And with that the window sash squeaked ever so softly in the night, and Gail came into the room. Not a man. No shining armor. But a knight in shining armor, nonetheless. And I was the damsel in distress.

Chapter 22

For a moment or two, I stopped breathing and just watched as Gail pulled herself like a cat burglar over the windowsill, as soundlessly as a cat itself.

The girl that stood in front of me was not the same girl that I had remembered from school. "What happened to you? You look so different."

"It's amazing how near starvation during this crazy apocalypse has really improved my physique. Best. Diet. Ever!" Gail whispered into Rose's ear, and pulled away to give her a genuine smile and a wink. "Now stop with the chatter. Let me get to work so that we can get you out of here."

I smiled back, nodding my head in understanding. This was not a funny giggling moment in the hallway at school. This was a life or death moment, and it needed to be over and done with as quickly as possible.

Reaching into her back pocket, Gail pulled out a large paper clip. She unbent it carefully, and knelt on the bed, trying to keep the bedsprings from squeaking. "Give me a minute with this," she said calmly as she took my handcuffed wrist in her hand. I closed my eyes- I hated when people watched me do things that required concentration- and prayed silently to myself. I could feel the twisting and turning of the paper clip in the lock, my stomach tying itself into knots with each twist. My imagination turned my stomach into a pet boa constrictor, and at first it seemed all well and good, but suddenly, my stomach, the snake, had turned on her, and I had no breath, suffocating.

And then suddenly I felt the strangulation release. Click. "Well, one down," Gail whispered, "now just one more handcuff lock to go. Hang in there."

This time, my stomach did not become the snake. The strangulation was not felt, but I still held my breath. This time, holding my breath like a kid before opening a present, anxious in anticipation. And then, the sweet release of breath with the sound of the click.

Freedom. Hope. Future.

"We need to get outside. We can't go through the house- too much risk of noise and squeaky floors." Gail pulled me slowly to my feet, and guided me to the window. "Just put your belly and head out first with one foot. Then, lower yourself slowly to the ground, feet first, holding on so that you don't drop and make a big rustling in the leaves. You first. I'm right behind you."

And with that, I moved like I was on the bomb squad. Not one unnecessary movement. Just careful, precise, measured actions towards our end goal. As I put my face out the window, the cold wind of the night whipped my hair into my eyes, forcing me into high alert. Easing my belly and leg onto the windowsill, I shifted and turned, belly now against the house, dragging my chest along the splintery shingles, and lowered myself down onto the ground below. Taking a step back, I looked up to the window, nodding to Gail.

Gail made short work of the same endeavor, gently guiding the window closed a bit more as she slid down the exterior of the house. "I took a second to just leave a lump in the bed, just in case they check on you in the night. Needed to look like someone was still there, at least until daybreak."

"Good thinking. So now what?

Gail held out her hand, and squeezed my hand. "Now we go get your brother."

Chapter 23

"Are you sure about this? I mean, I know we need to get my brother out of that house, but are you sure it's safe?" I murmured to Gail as we hugged the outside of the house, making our way along the perimeter in the shadows.

"Am I sure?" Gail asked. "I mean, no, I'm not sure. But, I am sure that Mr. Russell drinks himself into oblivion every night on his homemade moonshine liquor. I've been watching him very closely, even before you guys came along. He's gone to the world basically as soon as the moon starts to rise, passes out cold on the couch." Gail peeked around the corner, making sure the coast was clear. "Seriously, you'd have to drink yourself to sleep every night if you were doing what he's doing. Holding people against their will so that he can gobble up later, like pigs in a pen. You'd have to be drunk to escape your own guilty nightmares."

Gail squeezed my hand, and held up her other hand in a stop signal. Like a hawk listening for its prey in the swaying marsh grass, she held perfectly still before she made her next move.

"How'd you learn how to do that? Get the handcuffs off like that?" I whispered. "That was so cool."

Gail hesitated. "So cool? It's amazing how many cool things you can learn on YouTube during the hours, weeks, and years when all the other kids are hanging out with their friends. Being a friendless nerd and all, I used that time well. Guess my unpopularity just might've saved your life. And hopefully, your brother's." Her voice was quiet, hurt, like a sparrow's might be when awakening from the shock of hitting a window. A moment passed between us, and we both ducked in unison as a bat swooped down low over our heads in search of its buggy dinner.

"You're going to need to get Charlie's attention. Mr. Russell is out cold, presumably, in front of the fire as he does every other night, with Mrs. Russell sleeping next to him on the couch. Your brother is in the bedroom down the hall, but still close enough that we need to be careful."

"Get his attention? What should I do?" I questioned.

"Just whisper something in through the window, something so that quickly knows that it's you, so he won't be scared." Gail reached for my hands, "You can do this. You have to do this. I am going to get up into the room, just like I did with you, and free him from his handcuffs. Then, we're both going to get out of the window, just like you and I did already. Then we quickly and quietly head back to the trail. Trust me. Home free."

I paused. "Why are you risking your life for us? When I was so nasty to you?"

Bending in close to me, she put her forehead against my own. "Honestly, I couldn't live with myself otherwise. How could I just stand around in the shadows and watch you die? In school, with your friends, yes, you might have been a mean girl, but that doesn't mean that I could live with myself if I didn't try to help. To save your life. This isn't about wearing cool or uncool clothes. This is life or death." She could hear Gail take a deep breath, catching it in her lungs. "Now hustle. The sooner I get in there, the sooner we all get out."

I inched closer to the window, and seeing that it was open a crack, I leaned in and put my mouth as close as I could to the opening. "Hey Chucky, wanna play?" If Gail wanted me to let Charlie know quickly that it was me, I knew exactly what to say, an old line from an ancient 80s horror movie, using the nickname that he hated.

"Rose? Is that you?" Just hearing the fear in my brother's voice made me want to cry. What had that man already done to him?

"Charlie, it's me. I've got a friend with me. We're here to get you outta there. Stay quiet. She's coming in to get you out of the cuffs." I looked at Gail, and nodded at my former enemy to proceed with the plan. Gail hopped up onto the window sill, lifted the window open, and hauled herself inside.

"Keep watch," Gail whispered," I'll be as quick as I can."

It didn't seem possible that time could pass more slowly than when Gail was getting my own handcuffs off, but it did. Seconds turned into hours, minutes into days. How could they possibly escape before Mr. Russell came out of his drunken stupor or Mrs. Russell came to check on her in the middle of the night? What had seemed like an incredible idea now seemed incredibly foolish.

Waiting in the shadows, my mind flashed back to the last time I had actually seen Gail. It had been outside the principal's office, and Gail and her parents had just walked out, signing Gail out of school for the rest of the day. "Rose, please come in and take a seat," Miss Lester had said.

As I sat down, I looked down at the papers on the principal's desk. Printed copies of Instagram posts, fanned out like a cheap paper Chinese fan.

"Please hold my calls, Sheila. If you can get in touch with Rose's parents, please let them know that they need to come to the school right away." Miss Lester pulled the door closed behind her, and walked over to the mini-fridge in her office and got herself a water bottle. She settled down into her chair, adjusting the height of her chair so that she and Rose sat at the same level.

"So, Rose, what do you have to say for yourself? What's been going on with Instagram these days?" She shuffled the papers atop her desk into a nice neat pile, picking them up and tapping them into order.

"Miss Lester, it's nothing. It was just something funny. Seriously."

"Funny? Are you kidding me, Rose? How in the world did you think this was something funny? That this might be okay?"

Okay, so maybe I hadn't thought it was okay, but I certainly thought it was funny. Everyone did. And I had been so careful, had told everyone to be careful, so that no one else would see it. Even if it was ridiculously funny.

I had gotten the idea one day in science class, one when I had actually paid attention slightly. My science teacher was always kind of wacky, and while we were learning about stars and constellations, she had brought in these huge black pieces of paper with little dots splatter painted on them. During ancient times, she said that civilizations made pictures in the sky, constellations, to help them navigate and remember where certain stars were at certain times of year. She blabbered on and on about how kids these days, even if their lives depended on it for getting back home, would never be able to focus their attention away from their phones long enough to learn and remember such things.

Anyway, she had us gather all around her, and she played some music from her iPod. She asked us all to be quiet, to let our eyes relax and zone out on one of the painted papers, kind of like when we did those Magic Eye Illusions books. She asked us to just relax and see if we could create images by connecting the dots that we saw, much like George Lucas created Darth Vader's image from cliffside shadows formed in Zion Canyon. Then we played Pass the Pen, and we just silently traced out our own imaginary constellation images that we saw so that everyone else could see them, too. Some people traced out rabbits or puppies, while others saw cartoon faces and skyscrapers. After, we all got our own paper and paint to create our own little connect-the-dot scenes. It was cool; finally, for once, a cool science class.

"It was just something that I thought would be funny. I mean, I got the idea from science class, really, so you should really blame the science teacher."

"I can assure you, your science teacher had nothing to do with you creating an Instagram page called," she picked up the stacked papers on her desk for reference, "Connect the Dots- Do You See What I See?"

I had zoomed in and taken a picture of Gail from my class photo, zoomed in on her acne-covered face. Then, using Instagram tools, friends just copied and pasted the photo, connecting the dots on her zit-covered face to make pictures, constellations on her face. Gail the Whale. Gail the Snail. Gail in Jail. Gail's Got Mail. Gail's Gone Sailing. And my favorite, Gail's Turtle Tail.

"It just got out of hand. Gail was not supposed to ever see it. We didn't mean to hurt her feelings. It was just a joke." I rested my hands on the arms of my chair, afraid that my palms might leave sweatstains on my khaki pants if I put them in my lap.

"Well, surprise, surprise. She did see it, and so did her parents, after they spent the night in the hospital after she tried hurting herself after she'd discovered the Instagram posts. Really, I just don't know what was going through your head."

"I don't know, I got the idea after class, that's the truth, and then, I don't know, I just thought it would be wicked funny. Honestly, I didn't mean to hurt anyone, her. Really." I leaned forward, putting my hands together, almost in prayer. Little did I know, I was going to have to pray for a miracle if I ever wanted to see the inside of my school again.

"Really? Well, you may not have intended to hurt anyone, Rose, but you did. It's called the law of unintended consequences. Things happen even if you don't mean for them to. It's best to always think before you do things. Have a bit of foresight."

"So, now what? What's going to happen?"

"Well, maybe you should think about what you think is going to happen. We'll be making those decisions with your parents. Once they get here." Miss Lester looked down at the documents in front of her, leafing through the seemingly endless reams of paper, and just shook her head in silence, with a look of sadness on her face that made even me want to cry.

"You will not ruin this girl's life. Your laughter should not come at the expense of someone else, someone who is just trying to make it through each and every day without feeling like an outcast, like she doesn't matter. I will not stand by and let that happen." She swiveled around in her chair, like just looking at me was too much to bear, and stared out the window as we both waited.

The rest of that day was a bit of a blur- my parents coming to the school, discussion of expulsion proceedings, how to set up tutoring. Miss Lester didn't let me out of her sight, not until my parents brought me out to the car.

"What were you thinking? Why would you do something like that?" Her dad sat in the driver's seat, his head pressed against the steering wheel as they sat in the school parking lot.

"It was funny, I was just trying to be funny. Everyone thought it was. It's fine." I wrestled the cardboard box containing my locker's contents into the back seat.

"It's not funny. Even if other people think it is, it was just cruel." My parents stared back at me over the front seat. "Honestly," Dad continued, "that's not how we raised you." I remembered his sigh of disappointment, his quiet all the way home. Perhaps I had ruined his entire memory and belief of me, all for a bit of harmless fun. It was harmless, right?

"Hey, you there?" I snapped out of my memory zone, back to reality.

"Yup. Lower him down." I reached up, my heart leaping in my chest when I saw my brother's face light up when our eyes met. Guiding his feet down, I helped hold his legs as best as I could to help support him. When his feet finally touched down, he simply turned his body, and enveloped her in a big bear hug.

"Damn, it's good to see you, sis." I could feel my eyes start to well up with tears, and I caught myself. I gently guided him further along the side of the house and looked up, showing him with my eyes that Gail was already on her way down.

As Gail made contact with the ground, we welcomed her into our group hug. As our breathing slowed down, Gail raised her head from my tousled hair.

"Listen, kids, I'm all for a hug-a-thon, but we're not even close to being done yet. We still need to get out of town. Let's get a move on." Gail ruffled Charlie's hair, and we unfolded out of our hug, holding hands, the three of us. It was time to head home.

Chapter 24

Traipsing out of town beneath the moonlit sky, there was a peaceful calm. Barely a word passed between any of us, mostly for safety's sake than for anything else. Once we approached the border to the woods, I stopped in my tracks, and turned back to face the town.

"I can't believe what has happened to this place, to everything. And I was in such a rush to get back." I lay my head on Charlie's shoulder, taking a moment.

"Hey, you didn't know. Neither of us knew. What's done is done. No sense crying over spilled milk now." He grabbed my hand, heading single file into the forest, me trailing behind him.

"I could have I killed her when I hit her with that bedpan! What if I did permanent damage?" I froze, letting my face catch in the moonlight. A tear slowly dripped from the corner of my eye. "If I did, I would be just like them, killing, hurting so that I might survive. Just evil."

Gail sidled up next to me, putting her arm about my waist. "You did what you had to do. Even if you had killed her, it wouldn't have been on purpose. It would have been by accident. She was going to kill you on purpose, don't forget that. Big difference."

We continued on up the path, vigilant to the sounds around us. Two red squirrels skittering across our path nearly caused me to scream, but Charlie clapped his hand across my mouth before I got the chance.

"Can you find your way in the dark or do you want to rest instead?" Gail asked. "Since the EMP event, I haven't been up here much. Was afraid of what or who might lurk up here. Sounds funny, but it was easier to hide in town, nearly in plain view."

Charlie paused, taking in his surroundings, using the little light that the moon provided. "I think I just want to get back. Rose and I know these woods like the backs of our hands, and even though it's a bit tricky right now, it'll get easier as we get closer to home."

We hiked purposefully through the woods, Charlie taking note of leaves and paths on the forest floor. At times, he checked his direction by looking to the stars and moon, making sure that he had not gotten turned around in the dark of night.

Plodding along, we reached the lookout spot where we had stopped just yesterday. Stopped to take in the view of the town, where we had tried to make sense of the chaos that we spied from the elevated vantage point. We paused, huddled together side by side, with our arms about each other, looking down in the darkness at our town. At what could have been our last memory in our lives if things had turned out differently.

"Hey Gail, I just want to say I'm sorry for what happened back in school. I was a total jerk. Still not sure exactly why I did it, but I guess I was trying to be funny, and maybe the only way I thought I could be funny was to pick on someone else." I pulled Gail in even tighter into our side hug. "I'm not saying you have to forgive me, but I just wanted you to know that I'm sorry for what I did, for how it affected you." I gathered my thoughts for a second, "And now, here you are, risking your own life to save mine, after what I did to you. I just don't ever know how I could ever repay you." I squeezed us all together a bit tighter, sighing at the man at the moon, if he was indeed listening.

"Shhh... Do you hear that?" Gail whipped her head around, letting her eyes adjust to the view of the forest instead of the town down below in the valley. A distinct shuffling was coming toward us, a rustling in the leaves that wasn't from the wind. "Get down, bellies to the ground. Quick and quiet," she uttered beneath her breath.

Flattening ourselves like roadkill on the highway, we became invisible beneath the moonlight. Our breaths became shallow, slow. Our hearts nearly stopped in our chests, for fear that our heartbeats could actually be heard outside our bodies, like drumbeats.

A snap of a twig. A stumble in the leaves. A shuffle of regained footing. The sounds echoed across the forest floor to their ears like they were bats using echolocation to find their prey. But we were not the bat right now, but the prey instead.

And then it was silent. Not a sound, not even the wind, not even our own heartbeats in our heads. And then a whimpered song, barely discernible amidst sobbing.

"I've seen trees of green, red roses too, I've see them bloom, for me and you, and I think to myself, what a wonderful world." The voice barely carried through the air to our ears. "Oh my Rose, where are you?"

I felt Gail squeeze my hand. Wait.

I barely lifted my eyelids, watching in the moonlight for my father as he came down the path, singing the lullaby he had sung to me ever since I was a baby. Was he alone? Had somehow someone from town had found him and set him off to search for us? Was it a trap? My thoughts spun in circles, dragged into a downward spiral. Wait.

And then he came into view. He was alone. As he inched closer and closer to us hiding on the forest floor, I could tell. "And I think to myself, what a wonderful world," I echoed back to him in the best singing voice I could muster. Slowly rising, dusting the leaves from my hair and clothes, I went to him, hugging him tight like I was three and not thirteen.

I held my head to his chest, letting his fingers rake through my ponytail. "How's my girl? It's okay. Daddy's here now."

Letting my face catch the moonlight, I lifted my eyes to his. "Take me home."

Chapter 25

It had only been a day since we had left the farm, but it had felt like a lifetime. As the sun rose over the trees, it cast a hopeful glow on the new day.

Approaching the house, Dad squeaked the gate open, and Mom came bounding out the front door in her sheepskin slippers. "Oh, kids, I have been worried sick. Thank God you are home safe!" She wrapped her arms around both Charlie and me, pulling Dad in as she adjusted her robe and nightgown.

"Sorry to have been gone so long, Mom. We didn't mean to worry you," Charlie murmured between kisses to his cheeks and forehead.

"Mom, this is Gail. We had a few problems in town, and she helped us. Not sure what would have become of us without her help." I put my arm around Gail, bringing her into the family hug.

"Well, I'm just glad you are home safe," Mom said, pulling away and kissing my forehead and then Gail's hair. "Did you get the supplies from the list? Did you get your precious Doritos?"

Charlie, Gail and I all stole a glance at each other. "Actually, Mom, it's a long story. It's been a long day," Charlie chimed in.

"Well, you must be starving. Let's get you all some breakfast. What can I get for you, birthday girl?"

I put my arms out around everyone, putting my arms on the outside of the hug.

"Pancakes. I'm hungry for pancakes. Let's eat."

About the Author

Cirrus Farber grew up in Orleans, Massachusetts, a small seaside town on Cape Cod. She continues to live there now with her husband, Dawson, and their three children- a daughter, Madelyn, and identical twin boys, Lachlan and Grayson. For over 20 years, she has been an elementary school and middle school teacher. Besides cheering her kids on from the sidelines, she also enjoys singing, painting, mountain biking, reading, traveling, boating, paddleboarding, hiking with her black lab rescue pup, Pepper, and spending time on Nauset's outer beach with family and friends. <u>Off the Grid</u> is her first novel.

Made in the USA
Lexington, KY
08 November 2016